Other books by Kate Avery Ellison

The Curse Girl

Once Upon a Beanstalk

Frost (The Frost Chronicles #1)

Thorns (The Frost Chronicles #2)

Weavers (The Frost Chronicles #3)

Bluewing (The Frost Chronicles #4)

aeralis

KATE AVERY ELLISON

For everyone who loves the Frost and the characters who inhabit it.

AERALIS: THE FROST CHRONICLES #5

Lia Weaver and her friends have finally driven the Farther soldiers from the Frost, but the danger is not over yet. Ann Mayor and her father have found themselves the target of violence, the villagers are fighting, and Jonn's life hangs in the balance.

When an unexpected enemy surfaces in the Frost wilderness and endangers Lia's family, she faces a terrible choice, and against Thorns orders, she sets out to find answers in Aeralis.

PROLOGUE

"COME QUICKLY," IVY gasped. Her pale face glimmered in the darkness, and her pulse drummed against my fingers as I grabbed her wrist to steady her. "Jonn's collapsed."

"A seizure?" Anxiety fizzled through my veins. I released her and rushed for the door, dragging in lungfuls of air to clear my head before I went inside. He was overworked. He was pushing himself too hard. We should have seen this coming. I remembered how pale he'd looked when I'd retrieved him from our family's farm the day before. He'd practically fainted from exhaustion.

Ivy's voice made me freeze. She spoke low and fast, as if she didn't want anyone else to hear.

"Adam says he thinks it's the Sickness."

The Sickness.

The anxiety in my veins burst into flames of sheer panic.

I pushed through the doors and ran into the Assembly Hall with Ivy at my heels. People milled everywhere, murmuring quietly. The meetings had concluded for the day. Their faces showed no sign of alarm, so I assumed they didn't know. I shoved my way to the front of the room and found Ann waiting for me.

"Where is he?"

"They've taken him into the back," she said, and I ran for the door to the little alcove hidden away behind the dais before she'd even finished speaking.

This smaller room was dark, lit only by candles and a narrow window that let in moonlight. Jonn lay on the floor, his eyes shut, his hair a mess of sweat-soaked curls. Adam was crouched over my brother's still body, one hand pressed to the pulse at Jonn's throat. A Healer knelt at his side. The Mayor hovered nearby, watching.

"Lia," Adam said as soon as I came in, without raising his head. "Don't panic. He's all right, but we need to move him immediately."

"Ivy said—"

He shook his head without looking at me. Not here. I looked at the Mayor and clamped my lips shut as Ivy's words, words I couldn't say, shivered in my mind.

The Sickness.

Ivy slipped into the room and stood behind me without saying a word. She touched my arm. Her hands were cold.

"Where will we take him?" I asked.

"My house," Ann said, stepping through the doorway behind me and shutting the door after her. "We can quarantine him there. He'll be far from prying eyes. He'll be safe."

I nodded. Safe, and far from anyone he might infect.

Adam lifted him, and we went through the back door and out into the night. The cold Frost air nipped at my flushed face. Jonn moaned, and I reached for him.

"Try not to touch him too much," Adam said quietly.

I removed my hand.

Every step was excruciating. Jonn whimpered every time he was jolted, and I kept pace uselessly beside Adam and bit my lip until it bled. How had this happened? How had he become sick? It had been weeks and weeks since I had returned from the past.

We reached the Mayor's house. Ann opened the door, and we went inside. She led us to a guest bedroom on the top floor, one with a single bed in the corner and a high window on the wall that let in starlight. Adam ripped back the blankets with one hand and laid my brother on the bed with the other. I crouched beside the bed and rested my hand a few inches from Jonn's. Ivy was behind me, her lips pressed together to hold in a sob. The Healer joined Adam at the side of the bed, displacing me. I rose and went to a corner to pace. Ann stood in the doorway, watchful but keeping herself at a distance.

"Can we speak freely now?" I asked, looking at Adam.

He lowered his head and nodded. "We don't want to cause a panic, so the information must stay in this room, but I believe he has the Sickness. I've seen it before, and it is distinctive. This temporary coma, the sudden onset, the discoloration on his face. His pupils are dilated, he is feverish, and he was bleeding from his eyes and nose."

Ivy made a sound like a swallowed sob.

I crept closer to the bed where my brother lay without stirring. His skin was the color of snow, and dark bruises painted shadows beneath his closed eyes. His chest rose and fell rhythmically, and one of his fingers twitched against the bed.

"Are you completely certain he has it?" I asked.

"No," Adam said gently, as if the word could comfort me like a caress, as if that word should inspire me to hope. However, I could see in his expression that he was almost sure.

I took a deep breath. "If it is the Sickness...what do we do?"

"We quarantine him," Adam said. "It doesn't spread well in cold weather—that's why the Frost has always been protected—but someone else could get it if they weren't careful around him. We'll need to bathe carefully and burn the clothes we're wearing now to protect ourselves during his contagious period, which starts with the onset of the coma."

"And Jonn? What do we do for him?" My throat was tight.

"There is nothing that can be done for him now." He spoke gently but firmly. "We can only wait. If he recovers, he recovers. If he succumbs, he succumbs."

ONE

THE WIND OF the Frost whipped around me, making my cloak flutter and my cheeks prickle. I paused at the tree line, inhaling the scent of pine and ice and earth. Living in the village made me miss these things more than I ever realized I would, and I savored them now.

Ahead of me, Adam was a warm shadow of comforting silence as he waited for me to join him on the path that wove through the rocks and branches like a needle through a thick bunch of wool.

The snow crunched beneath my boots as I entered the Frost.

I reached his side, and we continued together, moving swiftly, not pausing to talk or catch our breath until we'd climbed the hill and reached the plateau where the sky dipped down and the mountains stretched up to mingle together on a darkening horizon. A faint shimmer touched the air, and I felt the energy straight to my bones.

Echlos.

Adam and I approached the entrance slowly, and when we had gotten within a few yards of the gaping hole that led inside, the shadows stirred and two figures stepped forward. The faces were almost identical, except one of the men had lighter, shorter hair than the other, and his face had an earnest quality while the other's expression was aloof, calculating, and cold.

"Gabe," Adam said. "Korr." It was not so much a greeting as an acknowledgement.

Gabe's eyes found mine, and I felt hot and cold. We hadn't seen each other in weeks, but it felt like years. Something about him was different. His hair was shorter now, cut into an Aeralian style, and his cloak and boots were of the finest material. But it wasn't those things. There was a new hardness to his eyes, a resolution and a fire.

He looked every inch the prince he was.

"Let's not waste time," Korr snapped. "Where is it?"

I looked at Adam, but he stepped back and gestured for me to lead the way. I started into the darkness, and they followed without a word. As the ruined grandeur swallowed us whole, I glanced over my shoulder at Korr's face. I wanted to see fear, or at least apprehension, but his expression was unreadable.

We climbed through darkness down to the bowels of the ruin, past crumbling walls and around piles of debris that half-barricaded the passages. Some of the walls were scrawled with unfamiliar symbols and letters, remnants of a time of chaos after Gabe and I had left. I remembered this place the way it had been—gleaming, all white stone and glass and quiet, echoing hallways filled with robed scientists and shy swabbers, who kept the floors shining and disappeared at the whistled signal that someone was approaching. I could almost taste the mingled scent of must and chemicals.

After endless sets of spiraling staircases and halls strewn with debris, we reached the room where the gate was kept. Our footsteps echoed as we entered. The edges of the ceiling disappeared into darkness, and through the hole in the roof, stars sparkled like shards of ice. At the end of the room lurked the gate, a sleeping gray circle.

"Is that it?" Korr asked, a note of suspicion in his voice. He surveyed the gate carefully, as if suspecting a trick.

"That's it," I said.

His expression revealed nothing. "And the PLD?"

I looked at Adam. We had promised it to Korr in exchange for his help driving the Farthers from the Frost, and besides, we no longer needed it. Still, I loathed giving it up, if only because it was a secret passed on to me by my parents, a secret that had been guarded by Weavers for hundreds of years.

Adam nodded slightly at me, his brow furrowing, and the meaning was clear.

We had no choice.

Korr lifted one eyebrow, expressing his impatience. "Don't make me list all the reasons you need to stay on my good side, Weaver."

Frustration simmered through my veins, but I steeled myself against it and crossed the room alone to the wall beside the gate. My fingers brushed the release for the secret compartment where Jonn had found the last of my father's journals, the one that had given him the instructions to operate the PLD. A panel slid aside, and a cylinder case glittered in the hidden alcove revealed beyond.

The portable locomotion device.

The case was cold and heavy in my hands as I returned to the others.

Korr snatched it from me. He opened the flap and withdrew the device—a long, thin metal pipe with wires sprouting from one end. He didn't say anything as he probed it. After a thorough examination, he tucked the PLD into a pouch beneath his cape, and as simply as that, it was gone from me.

"I'm not sure what use you think you can derive from the device," I said. "The gate is still set to take travelers back to the past. We don't know how to change it."

Korr seemed unruffled by my words. He smoothed his cloak with a flick of his fingers and regarded me with a frosty glare. "It's time that we took our leave. Little brother?"

Gabe met my eyes instead of Korr's. "Ready," he said, but the word was a sigh.

"We have more to discuss, but let's get out of this forsaken place before the monsters eat us," Korr muttered, and turned on his heel for the exit.

We headed back for the surface, and once again I was drowning in memories of Echlos's past, both recent and ancient—stark white corridors filled with scientists and hissing gates delivering jumpers, and the same corridors centuries later, filled with fugitives in my care, huddled together against the cold as we struggled to survive the harsh climate.

Gabe's steps deliberately slowed to match mine, letting Korr and Adam get ahead of us. We looked at each other out of the corners of our eyes, but we didn't speak. It'd been three weeks since I'd seen him last, three weeks since the night when he'd kissed me and then vanished into the night after our defeat of the Aeralian soldiers. Three weeks of time and an eternity of worry and pain.

"How are you?" he asked in a low voice.

I hesitated, focusing on my feet instead of looking at him. A flood of words pushed at my lips, threatening to spill out—how I'd paced and wept at the news of Jonn's sickness, how the village people fought over everything from new quota laws to who could rightfully call themselves a Frost dweller, how I missed him and the ache was like a bruise on my heart. But he had left us. Things had changed. I didn't know what I could say to him anymore. He was Gabe, my friend, but an aura of otherness clung to him like a garment, and he was working with Korr now. The familiarity we'd once shared was tainted by unease.

"Life is still a perilous dance," I said finally.

"You are the Bluewing." Something glimmered in his eyes. Regret? Desire?

"How is Aeralis?" I asked after casting about for something else to say, desperate to fill the space between us that was now laden with pain. "Where are you living?"

Gabe ran a hand over his newly shorn hair. "A slum. All crumbling stone buildings and clouds of steam from the factories."

"Not in Korr's fancy house?"

He shook his head. "I can't be seen with my brother, because I'd be recognized at once for who I am, and by all accounts I'm dead. I have to stay away from his usual venues and anyone who might know me—or Korr, since our resemblance is obvious—which rules out all the nice places. Even his home is off limits, since Korr's involvement is one of our greatest secrets, given his closeness to the Dictator. I've been living with another Restorationist."

"Restorationist?"

"It's what we're called, because we want to see the old monarchy restored."

"And your family? Any news of them since you've returned to Aeralis?"

He bit his lip and looked away. "Korr smuggled them away in secret once he solidified his standing with the Dictator. I won't be able to see them again unless we overthrow him."

"At least they're alive," I managed.

"Yes," he agreed.

All small talk ran dry between us after that, and again the air shivered with unspoken things as our footsteps crunched over debris that littered the ruins. My heart ached with hurt and regret, and I was brimming with words that I refused to say. Why had he left so suddenly? Why did he trust his brother now? Why could we find nothing to say to each other except stilted talk of revolutions?

"I miss you." The words came out unexpectedly, and I flushed. I hadn't meant to say them.

I saw his chest rise and fall, and his neck flushed. Then he said, almost so low I missed it, "Come back with me."

I bit my lip. "That's impossible."

"I know you said no before, but things were unsettled. The Frost had just been liberated. Now, however—"

"I can't. It's impossible to even consider."

"Lia—"

"Jonn has the Sickness." It burst out of me, the declaration fueled by pain and sadness and anger rolled up together.

"What?" Gabe said sharply, stopping. "The *Sickness*? How?"

I kept walking doggedly, and he caught my arm and pulled me around. I shot a glance ahead at Korr and Adam. They lingered at the end of the hall, watching us. Adam's eyebrows lifted as he took in my expression, and he narrowed his eyes at Gabe.

I shook my head slightly to communicate that I was all right. I didn't want Korr making inquiries, so I resumed walking as I answered Gabe's questions in whispers.

"I don't know how it happened," I said. "He's been quarantined. He's been in a coma of sorts since it happened. We're simply waiting." *Waiting for him to die,* but I didn't say that. I refused to say that.

Regret and horror mingled in Gabe's eyes. "I'm so sorry. I didn't know, or I would have—" He swallowed. "What are you going to do?"

"There's no cure."

"Perhaps the doctors in Aeralis—"

"No cure," I repeated, my voice harsh.

Silence fell between us. Gabe's shoulders slumped. His eyes slid away from mine. "I'm sorry," he whispered. "He was like a brother to me, too."

We reached the entrance to Echlos and went out into the cold. The night sky glittered above us, the black punctured with stars. Gabe fumbled with his cloak while I squinted at the stars and the silence crawled over me.

"Gabe," I began.

"Listen," he interrupted, and his voice held a note of earnest desperation that silenced me. "If you ever—I mean, if you reconsider—" He stopped, gathering his dignity, and this time when he spoke, his words were measured and calm. "If you ever find yourself in Aeralis and you need to find me, come to the Plaza of Horses. There's a statue there of a stallion with one leg outstretched. Leave a message in its mouth—there's a hollow place where the iron has rusted away—or wait beneath it. I'll look for you."

"Gabe." The only way I'd conceivably find myself in Aeralis was if I took him up on his offer and came with him, and that would never happen.

"Just remember," he said.

I sighed. "I'll remember. Plaza of Horses. Statue of a stallion."

"Weaver," Korr snapped, with the impatience of a man who was not accustomed to being ignored. "Has starvation wasted away your hearing along with the rest of you? I asked you a question."

Gabe and I had been so engrossed in our conversation that we'd almost forgotten about them.

I straightened and crossed my arms.

"What do you want, Korr?"

His mouth slid into a smile that might have been called charming if it had been on anyone else's face. "I hear your father has a magnificent collection of journals and notebooks," he said. "I would like to purchase them from you."

"Absolutely not." I wasn't letting him anywhere near my father's precious notebooks, which chronicled the secrets and histories of my family in addition to my father's personal struggles, hopes, and fears.

Korr arched one eyebrow. "I think you'll find me quite generous."

"They're not for sale."

"Surely there is something you want," he purred.

"No," I said. "And why do you want them, anyway?"

"Call me a collector of curiosities," he said.

My gaze fell on the PLD in his hand, and I understood. "The device was part of our deal; information about its origin and use was not. You'll have to discover it on your own."

"Come now," he said, cajoling.

I glared at him. "You haven't a chance of convincing me."

"You're making a mistake," he said. "Don't be stupid, Weaver. I could do a lot for this miserable excuse for a civilization you have here."

"Stop insulting me, or I'll summon the Watchers," I snapped.

At that, Korr paled. He had no defense against the monsters that roamed our wilderness, unlike Adam, Gabe, and me. My family lineage protected me, and both Adam and Gabe had been injected with a serum that would turn the monsters away. However, Korr was defenseless.

His mouth twisted, but then he smiled.

"I'll concede to you the battle," he said. "But not the war. Sooner or later, Lia Weaver, I'll have something you want."

His eyes slid to Gabe as he spoke the last few words, and I didn't react, but my heart thudded. I didn't trust this man not to use everything I cared about to get what he wanted from me, even if he had to betray his own flesh and blood. But I wasn't giving that snake my father's notebooks.

"Let's go, Gabriel," Korr snapped.

Gabe leaned close and put his lips to my ear.

"I'll look for you."

We parted without goodbyes. I watched until Gabe and his brother vanished from view among the trees.

Once they'd gone, Adam and I headed for Iceliss.

If you ever are in Aeralis and you need to find me, come to the Plaza of Horses.

The invitation haunted me.

"I hope I never have to see that man again," I muttered.

Adam looked at me but said nothing. A faint smile touched his mouth, and I scowled.

"What is it?"

He shook his head. "I just enjoy seeing the lord brought to speechlessness, that's all."

We shared a grim smile as we reached the path that lead to the village, and a comfortable silence filled the space between us. Adam didn't ask what Gabe had whispered to me, but I think he wanted to.

"Have you managed to contact the Trio yet?" I asked. Since the liberation of the Frost, he'd been sending messages with no response.

"No," Adam said. "I am still waiting. I shall continue to try to reach them."

Gabe's final words continued to echo in my mind. *I'll look for you.*

We reached the hill and descended the path to Iceliss's main gate. The village had changed in the last few weeks. The Farther additions remained, but we'd strung the skeletal reminders of our captivity with garlands of snow blossoms and hung them with ribbons. The walls still stood as well, but they were empty of soldiers. Wreaths of pine hung on every door, celebratory symbols of our victory. And everywhere I looked, embroidered banners of a blue bird called the bluewing danced and furled in the wind.

Bluewing—my alias during my exile from the village and civilization, and the name I'd used as I'd made plans to drive the Aeralian occupiers out of the Frost. It had become a symbol of freedom, a symbol of the Frost itself.

Adam and I traveled in silence to the former Mayor's house, where Ivy and I were still staying. Someone had strung ribbons on all the trees, and they fluttered in the wind. I climbed the steps to the front door, and weariness settled in my bones.

Before we went inside, Adam's fingers caught mine, and he turned me around to face him. He scanned my face, his mouth saying nothing, his eyes asking everything. The pressure of his hand against mine stirred heat inside me. He'd refrained from speaking about us as a couple the last few weeks—we'd been so busy with the new liberation, and Gabe's sudden and abrupt disappearance had left me wounded and confused.

Now I'd seen Gabe again, and the meeting had sent me into a melancholy silence.

Neither of us spoke as he searched my eyes. He touched my cheek once, a gesture meant to be comforting rather than romantic, I supposed, although it still sent shivers over my skin. Wordlessly, he opened the door and went inside. I followed.

A shape stirred in the warm darkness, and a match flared to life. Ann. She lit a lamp and padded forward to greet us.

"Did you see them?"

"The PLD has been delivered," I said.

Her eyes shifted to Adam, and he tipped his head to the side. "They both looked well," he said, answering the question she didn't ask.

"Oh," she said. "Good."

Silence wrapped us all in invisible bonds. Ann harbored some strange connection with Korr, forged over the months of her captivity in Aeralis. I didn't understand it.

"We should get to bed," she murmured after I said nothing.

Adam's glance was like a caress. "I'll see you in the morning."

They left me. I climbed the ornate central staircase and turned left. I stopped at the end of the hall, before a door hung with black ribbons. It was the sign for sickness. In this case, *the* Sickness.

One of the Healers sat outside the door, dressed in a white tunic. She glanced up at me, saying nothing.

"How is he?" I asked.

"The same."

He'd been sleeping for weeks, his thin body struggling with every breath, his lungs rasping, his skin the color of old milk, his lips cold and pale as frost on a windowpane. His eyelids, closed and threaded with bulging veins, fluttered but never opened.

I rested my forehead against the door and shut my eyes. Inches of wood and miles of silence separated us.

"Please wake up," I whispered.

Silence.

With a sigh, I turned to go to my room.

Ivy shared the vast featherbed with me. So much had changed for us in such a short time. My little sister, always the baby, the troublemaker, had blossomed into an astonishing leader when it came to the Watchers. She lay curled in a fetal position beneath the feather-stuffed white comforter, her hair fanned across the pillow, her cheeks flushed with the warmth of sleep. I slipped in beside her, moving slowly so as not to wake her. Her face, slack with unconsciousness, was almost angelic in sleep.

Two sleeping siblings.

But one might not wake up.

Tightness squeezed my throat. I turned over, pulled the blankets over my head, and shut out the world with my eyelids.

A pounding sound far away woke me hours later. The room was dark as pitch, the air icy above the quilt. My confusion turned to anxiety as I heard Adam's voice in the hall, and I threw back the blankets and ran to the door.

Adam stood in the hall, his eyes on the foyer below, his mouth pressed in a line.

"What's wrong?" My heart pounded. My stomach was sick with dread. "Who is it?"

He shook his head to show he didn't know.

I grabbed my cloak to wrap around my sleep clothes and followed him into the hall. The sound of shouting floated up from the foyer. Adam and I exchanged a glance. I heard Ann's name as well as the former Mayor's, along with strings of ugly epitaphs and the sound of fists pounding on the door.

Ann stood by the stairs, wrapped in a robe. She stepped from the shadows as we descended to the foyer, and I wrapped both arms around her. Dark circles shadowed the hollows beneath her eyes, and her lips were pressed in a thin, brave line.

Adam strode across the room and wrenched the door open. Lantern light outlined the bodies of the people on the porch and spilled across the floor. I could make out no individual faces in the darkness.

A mob.

TWO

"WHAT DO YOU want?" Adam demanded. His voice was harsh from sleep and anger, and he spoke with the full force and authority of his position as Thorns leader.

"We want the Mayor and his girl gone," someone shouted. "They don't deserve to live in this fine house anymore, enjoying luxuries the rest of us cannot. They're traitors!"

Traitors? Who dared to say such things?

I shoved past Adam and glared into the face of the man who'd spoken. I recognized him—a Tanner. He hadn't been involved in the liberation of the Frost. He'd been one of the ones who'd hidden in their home, one of the ones who wasn't injected with the serum that kept the Watchers away.

"Ann Mayor has done more for this town than you," I said. "She helped defeat Raine. She risked her life. That's more than I can say for you, Robert Tanner."

He flinched at the mention of his name. "If her father hadn't sold us to the enemy, there would have been no Raine."

"You're a coward," I said. "Coming here now, making these accusations in the dark of night—"

The Tanner sneered at me. "You know as well as I that the Mayor family has wronged us all. They don't deserve to stay here in this fancy house. They don't deserve to be in Iceliss at all. We want them gone, or we'll burn down the house."

Anger boiled in my veins. "Get off this porch," I said. "This is a mob. This is not how we do things here. We can meet to discuss this in daylight when I can see all your faces properly."

"You're the Bluewing," he said. "I respect that. But you're wrong to harbor her. We'll see justice done."

"Daylight," I repeated. "I won't be cowed by a mob."

I remained in the doorway until they left the porch, then I shut the door and leaned against it, shaking. I wasn't shaking with fear, though, but with anger.

I looked at Ann. Her lips trembled as she spoke. "They have every reason to—"

"No. I won't hear you defend their prejudice and hate. How dare they ignore your role in the liberation? Your father's role?"

"My father's role is the only reason why he wasn't shot that night."

I chewed my lip and growled in frustration.

"I've expected this," she continued. "I knew they'd come. They've been looking at me as if I were a snake since the liberation."

"You're a hero," I snapped.

"They don't really know that. All they know is that I'm a Mayor. My father—"

"You are not your father!"

"That mob doesn't care," she said. "And I think they're right about one thing. I think perhaps I should leave."

"Absolutely not—"

"Lia," Adam said firmly. "Ann is right."

I stared at him, shock silencing me.

"She should leave for her own safety," he said. "I was thinking perhaps she and her father could stay temporarily at the Weaver farm, now that it's been returned to your family's possession."

The farm. I saw it in my mind's eye, blanketed in fresh snow, far from the village and this madness.

My blood buzzed in my ears as if I'd swallowed a thousand bees. My hands itched to break something. "All right," I said after a pause. "But I hate this. It's stupid. It isn't fair."

"Maybe not," Ann agreed. "But it's what I have to do."

~

Ivy and I helped Ann carry her things to the farm, and I settled her into my old room. Being back felt like a dream—similar to my memories, but different. Some of the furniture had shifted, a thick coat of dust covered the tables and shelves, and the walls felt tighter around me. It was as if I'd grown in size, or the house had shrunk. I trailed my hand across the top of my bureau, leaving streaks in the wake of my fingertips.

Ann kept her mouth fixed in a smile, but I could see the glimmer of apprehension that shimmered in her eyes as she looked through the window at the yard and the Frost beyond.

"You've both been injected with serum," I said quietly as I knelt to help her unpack her things. "Watchers won't attack you if they get a whiff of your blood. Remember that."

"Yes. Too bad bears don't respond to the serum as well." Ann reached into her luggage and began pulling out cloaks and dresses. She crossed the room to the bureau and opened a drawer. She dumped the things inside and stopped, lowering her head. "I'm scared, Lia."

"We don't get many bears this close to the village."

Ann giggled, a half-hysterical sound. She shut the drawer and turned to face me. "It isn't as if I haven't lived out in the wilderness before. I don't know why I'm being such a mouse about it."

It was true—she'd spent several weeks with us as a fugitive in the Frost ruins, but she'd never been on her own with only her father for company.

"But this time..." She stopped. "I'm not a traitor, Lia."

"I know."

She chewed her lip. "It will be lonely here."

"I'll visit you," I promised. "We're not abandoning you."

She nodded slowly and went to unpack the rest of her things.

"I'll see how your father is coming," I said.

Below, I found Ivy building a fire while the former Mayor watched with fascination and apprehension. I realized with bemusement that neither Ann nor her father had probably done much—if any—household work. They'd always had servants for that. Well, no longer.

The sight of the warm wooden walls and narrow, shuttered windows made my chest ache with longing to stay. I missed this place to my bones, but my work was far from done. They needed me in the village.

"Thank you for your assistance," the Mayor murmured to Ivy. He looked away from me, and I realized he was afraid of me now.

Ann descended the stairs and looked at us, then the fire. Silence fell over the room.

"We should get back to the village," Ivy said softly.

Ann crossed the room and hugged me. I clung to her a moment, squeezing her tight to reassure myself that she was safe, that she was going to be all right here without me, without any protection. Despite my assurances to her earlier, I was worried.

"We'll be fine," she whispered, as if reading my thoughts.

Ivy and I left the house and started across the yard. I listened to the sound of our boots squishing in the sludge of melting snow and inhaled the scent of pine and wet earth.

"It's stupid," Ivy muttered without looking at me.

"Yes," I agreed, and I wondered when my sister and I had stopped fighting and started sharing the same thoughts and opinions. We were shoulder to shoulder as we walked, and I realized she was almost as tall as I was. She was almost a woman now.

I stopped by the barn.

"You go on," I told Ivy. "I have something I need to do."

The barn door creaked as I shoved it open. Sunlight illuminated the space, catching dust motes and making them sparkle. The air smelled of must and old hay, and I sneezed as I stepped around scattered farm tools. I crossed the room to the compartment in the floor that led to the lower room beneath the barn, the one where my parents had kept their secret life as Thorns agents and Weaver heritage keepers hidden from us.

My fingers automatically found the button concealed among the stones, and the door slid open with a rusty scraping sound. I descended the steps, stopping to feel my way through the dark. I fumbled for the matches I'd left the last time. I struck one against the stone wall, and it flared and sputtered in the darkness. I lit a lantern and sank down among the boxes and stacks of books.

"I wish you were here, Ma," I whispered aloud. "Jonn is sick."

Silence hung in the space around me, thick as the dark the lantern light kept at bay. My words withered and fell away unheard.

He was dying, and I was helpless to save him. I would do anything, but there was nothing to be done.

Sighing, I reached for one of the boxes and lifted the lid to peer inside. It contained stacks of papers, all old documents belonging to my parents. Lists of names, maps, catalogs of supplies. I sifted through them, feeling the brittle paper between my fingers, gazing at the scrawl of my father's handwriting.

At the bottom of the box lay a wooden case. I picked it up and turned it over in my hand. A jewelry box—my mother's jewelry box. Why was it in here with the papers and documents? She'd kept it in her dresser drawer, beneath her underthings and stockings. As a child, I'd loved to sift through the sparkling pieces and rub them until they shone clean. Rings, earrings, all my mother's treasured family heirlooms. Memories rushed over me.

My fingers slipped, and the box crashed to the floor. Strands of silver scattered. Brooches tumbled out. I righted the box quickly, carefully replacing each piece.

Something protruded from the corner of the box where the velvet lining was pulling away from the wood. A paper of some sort. The fall of the box must have dislodged it.

I tugged gently at the scrap, and a folded square of paper slid into my hand.

A letter.

I unfolded it and scanned the first line.

My dearest Lia, Jonn, and Ivy,

I stopped. My heard pounded. This letter was meant for us.

I unfolded the rest of the paper and spread the sheet out on my lap. My lips moved as I read the words silently.

There is something you need to know, something I've not yet had the courage to tell you.

First, let me tell you a story.

Lia and Jonn—when you both were small, before Jonn's injury, before Ivy was even born, a fugitive found his way to our farm. He was Aerialian, running from the injustice of a wrongful accusation. This was before the royal family had been deposed, before the Aerialians became the Farthers we know today. He was from a farm on their plains, a man who loved woods and sky and snow as much as any Frost dweller. We granted him refuge, and he lived in our barn. He even helped us build the secret room that lies below the floor, a place where he could live in safety.

I stopped reading and looked around me at the room in wonder.

Your father was always fascinated with the remains of the Weaver legacy that we've written about in the journals. He began uncovering ruins, making maps, finding books and inventions that he could not understand. He would make long trips into the Frost, searching for answers, uncovering everything he could find. The Frost held many treasures, many secrets, and he found many of them.

Then, one day more than a month after the fugitive had joined our little farm, your father

The rest of the letter was missing. I turned it over, but there was nothing written on the other side. I examined the jewelry box and sifted through the papers I'd found it with, but there was no sign of the rest of the letter.

I folded the paper and slipped it into my pocket as the words swirled in my mind, haunting me.

There is something you need to know, something I've not yet had the courage to tell you.

What was it?

THREE

THE JOURNEY BACK to Iceliss melted into a blur as the sharp white of snow and the jagged cuts of green spun around me. My mother's words sparked in my brain, and with every remembrance, my mind spun with questions,

There is something you need to know.

I reached the Cages and passed beneath the snow blossom-trimmed bars. The flower-wreathed metal striped me in shifting shadows, and I shivered reflexively. We might cover them with beauty, but the reminder of all we'd lost remained. Some of the flowers were already withering, revealing the steel beneath once more. It looked more like a memorial to honor something long dead rather than a celebration.

Beneath our attempts to cover them, the truth showed through like bones.

Something I've not yet had the courage to tell you.

In the village streets, a crowd had gathered. Shouts split the air. I pushed my way through the clusters of men and women, trying to make out the furtive whispers as I elbowed my way to the middle of the commotion.

Two men shoved at each other in the center of the crowd. Their eyes were bright and sharp with fury, and their mouths spat accusations. Their cloaks fluttered as they circled each other.

"What is going on?" I shouted.

The men drew apart and looked at me, and their fury faded as they recognized my face. One was a villager, a

Fisher. The other was one of the fugitives that had returned with me through the gate.

"Bluewing," the fugitive said. "We—"

"I should not have to share my quota with an outsider!" the Fisher snarled. "They've brought us nothing but confusion and trouble. There's even talk of disease spreading."

A hot wave swept through me, obliterating any sense of tact I might have.

"Shut up," I said, and the words came out cold and cutting.

They both fell silent and looked at me. And they listened, respect in their eyes, because I was Bluewing. Surely, I would know what to do. The mockery of their trust when I felt so lost made me brittle inside. I wet my lips with my tongue and gathered words to soothe them.

"We were all outsiders once," I said. "And those who live among us now helped bring us peace."

"But the rumors of illness—"

"They deserve our respect and thanks. We're all in this together now."

The man looked away.

"Bluewing—" someone began in protest.

"Do you remember how we ended up in the grip of the Farthers?" I shouted. "Do you remember how it grew worse and worse? We were fragmented, suspicious. We were at each other's throats. It was so easy for them to take us. We were weak, and we will continue to be weak if we continue to fight and mistrust and hate."

Mutters swirled in the air around me. I stared at each man in turn, willing them to hear the words I spoke and take them to heart, and then I turned and headed for the former Mayor's house in the center of town.

~

Adam was waiting on the porch when I reached the house. The wind caught his cloak and made it flutter. His eyes were dark and full of unspoken things as they met mine.

"We need to talk."

Apprehension brewed in my stomach, and the questions raised by my mother's letter fled my mind. I climbed the steps to meet him.

"What is it?" My voice came out low, emotionless. Adam didn't have many expressions that he wore openly, but I detected his apprehension in the way his eyes tightened and his fingers twitched. Whatever his message, he was loath to deliver it.

Adam tipped his head to the side, considering me, weighing his words. "I've made contact with the Trio at last. I've received our orders."

I breathed out. This did not pertain to Jonn, at least.

"And?"

"I've been given orders to help with the liberation effort in Aeralis. I'm to leave for Astralux right away."

The world telescoped around me as I absorbed his words. "What?"

Adam didn't repeat himself. He knew I'd heard him the first time. He just stood there, letting it sink in, letting me process it.

"What about me?" I managed.

His expression softened almost imperceptibly. "The Thorns think you're best suited to remaining here as a contact, and I think it's best, too. The villagers listen to you. They look to you for guidance."

"But—"

"Stay here and look after your brother."

I'd just lost Gabe, and Jonn was at death's door. How could I stand to lose Adam, too? How could I do this alone?

"I don't want you to go." The words ripped themselves from me in a moment of sheer weakness.

Adam's eyes fluttered half-closed, and his lips pressed together in the way they always did when he wanted to speak but refrained from doing so. I saw frustration—and understanding—mingled in his eyes.

I brushed past him for the house. Adam remained outside. I shut the door behind me and leaned against it. I tried to breathe deeply to calm myself, but my throat was squeezing too tight.

How could the Trio ask Adam to walk away from the Frost when it was as weak and new as a fresh-born baby?

~

After shutting myself in the room I shared with Ivy, I took the paper from the place where I'd wadded it into my belt and put it in the drawer of the bureau beside the bed. I fell back against the quilt and stared at the cracked plaster ceiling. Slowly, my vision began to blur, and I heard her whispering to me. My mother. Her voice was soft and warm, and I felt whole and well for the first time in weeks.

"Don't be afraid," she said. "You're strong, Lia. You're a Weaver."

"I miss you, Ma," I whispered. "I don't know what to do."

I turned my head. She sat on the bed beside me, and she was so beautiful even in the darkness. Light glimmered like stars in her hair, and her smile was pure grace. She opened her mouth to speak.

"Wake up, Lia."

It was Ivy's voice.

I lifted my head from the pillow and squinted at Ivy's face in the near-darkness of early morning. I'd been dreaming.

My limbs still ached with weariness, and my eyes were gritty with sleep. "What is it?" I curled my fingers around the edges of my pillowcase and wished for sleep, because with sleep came oblivion. With sleep came dreams.

"It's Jonn. The Healer says to come."

Jonn. The fog of sleep vanished. I threw back the covers and swung my legs over the side of the bed as dread sunk into my gut. "What's wrong? What's happening?"

"I don't know. They only said to fetch you at once."

She darted from the room like a nervous bird, and I followed, my mouth dry and my breath snagged in my throat.

Adam was waiting outside the door to Jonn's room, conversing with one of the Healers, a young woman. I slowed as I reached them, Ivy at my back.

"How is he?" The words stuck in my throat. I forced them out.

The Healer spoke. "He's awake."

Ivy gasped. "Awake? As in he's getting better?"

I made no sound. Awake, as in *not dead*. I put out a hand to steady myself against the wall.

The Healer didn't smile. Her mouth moved, but I no longer heard what she said. My brother was awake. That had to mean something good.

"Can I see him?" I found myself asking, interrupting her.

The Healer looked at Adam before replying. "We do not know everything about the cycle of the disease, but from the books you've provided for us from the Ancients, his period of contagiousness has passed."

I already had my hand on the door.

"Wait," Adam said, and his voice broke through to me. "Lia, you...you should listen to her."

I looked at the Healer, impatient.

"He is awake," she said, "but he is not recovered." She paused, seeing that I didn't understand. "He is still dying, Lia."

All the air sucked from my lungs as the words hit me, a punch in the gut, a bruise forming around my heart and spreading to my limbs. I breathed in and out, a raspy sound in the sudden silence. Ivy's hands grabbed for me, and we swayed together in silence, two sisters absorbing one terrible blow. I was glad she was with me in that moment; I didn't know if I could have faced it alone.

Ivy whispered, "Please, can we see him?"

"Yes, but don't overtire him," the Healer said, and this time her voice was gentle. She'd delivered her hard news; now all that was left was helping us put ourselves back together. "Go one at a time. It'll be less overwhelming for him that way."

"You first," Ivy said, and I turned the knob and went into the room. The door clicked shut behind me.

I was alone with my brother.

My eyes crawled over the floor, the walls, and the window before landing on the central thing: Jonn. He was swathed in quilts to his chin, his body just a narrow bump beneath the covers. He looked young, fragile, like a little boy waiting for his mother to come and kiss him goodnight. At the sound of my footsteps on the wooden floor, his eyes fluttered open. He looked at me and tried to smile, but his mouth seemed broken.

I took a few steps, breathing the stale air that stank of sickrooms and sweat and uneaten soup. Each step took a lifetime. Each step, time bled away too fast.

Dying.

I reached his side and stopped. My hands hovered over him, and I was reluctant to touch him and aching to at the same time. I rested one hand hesitantly over the lump of his shoulder beneath the blanket.

"Jonn," I said gently.

His voice was just a croak. "Lia."

Silence hovered between us as I sank down to the chair beside him. I clasped my hands in my lap. "How— how do you feel?"

"The way I must look," he said, and laughed under his breath. It turned into a cough, and I saw flecks of blood on the blanket as he bent over it.

"Jonn—"

"It's fine." He straightened, still gasping for air, wheezing as he sucked life into his lungs and blew it out again. "They won't tell me anything yet. How are you and Ivy? How is Adam? The village? How is everyone adjusting to the liberation? What's happened since I've been out?"

I thought of the letter I had hidden in the bureau drawer. I flinched.

Jonn raised his eyebrows.

"We're fine," I said. "Worried about you, of course, but keeping busy. Everything is different now, and no one knows exactly how to take it. There's been a great deal of disagreement already."

"I can imagine." He brought his hands up from under the quilts and rested them over his chest, folded, corpse-like. I averted my gaze from them, looking instead at his eyes. His pupils were constricted and veins bulged around the irises.

"They demanded that Ann and the Mayor—the former Mayor, I mean, well, Ann's father—leave the village."

"What? Leave? Where are they now?"

"Staying at our farm." I paused. "But I'm worried about them. It isn't a permanent solution. Then there's the matter of Echlos and the PLD. We saw Korr and Gabe days ago, and I handed it over to them, but I don't feel—" I stopped. "Is this all right? Am I exhausting you?"

He moved his fingers in a gesture that perhaps was meant to be reassuring, but it looked like a cat clawing for a bird. "I'm all right. I want to know what's happening. I'll go insane if I don't."

"Adam is leaving." I said it quietly, my head lowered.

"What?"

"He's been ordered to join Korr and Gabe in Aeralis. The Trio wants it."

He exhaled heavily. One hand plucked at the quilt. "And you?"

"I'm to stay here and help the villagers, Adam says. Keep them from killing each other." My voice betrayed the defeat I felt.

Jonn raised his eyebrows. "I thought you were no longer under Adam's authority," he said, with a hint of his old spark. "I thought he said he was going to let you continue leading here as you'd been doing. Doesn't that mean you're no longer bound to do what he says if you disagree?"

"I'm still a member of the Thorns. I still get orders from the Trio. Besides, I have no desire to go to Aeralis and work for Korr." I hesitated. "I don't want him to leave, though."

Jonn absorbed this information. "Who's fighting? What's wrong in the village?" he asked.

"People are worried," I said, speaking carefully now. I didn't want to alarm him. "There are disputes about quota, about sharing what we have with the newcomers among us. Some are talking about illness. They don't know that the Sickness has come again, but they're worried. Some are blaming the Aeralians in our midst. They want them gone in case more become infected."

"It hasn't come again," Jonn said. "Not like that. Besides, it wasn't the fugitives' fault."

"But how did you contract it? It must have come from somewhere." I stopped. *It wasn't the fugitives' fault*, he'd said, as if he knew the real source. "Whose fault is it?"

Jonn cleared his throat. "Mine. I contracted the disease on...on purpose."

I rose from the chair. "What are you talking about?"

"I read it in one of our father's notebooks. Those who contracted the disease but didn't die—they were stronger, better. They recovered from disease and injury. They were new again. Whole. No longer crippled."

My throat was dry. My tongue stuck to my teeth as horror filled me. "What are you saying?"

"The package I asked you to bring me from Borde." He traced one finger in slow circles over the quilt across his chest. "It was a dead mouse, infected with the Sickness. I handled it, allowed myself to become sick. But no one else will. I burned the corpse, and I've been quarantined."

I was shaking. Shaking with horror and rage. "How could you do this? To Ivy? To me? To all of us!"

He just looked at me, and I read the anguish in his eyes.

"Everiss is dead, Lia. I have a wasted leg, I get sick often, I have seizures. I'm weak. There's no place for me in this world."

"That isn't true!"

"I'm weak," he insisted. "Too weak."

"So you decided to kill yourself?"

"With any luck, I'll recover and be stronger. Healed..."

"Jonn, you're dying."

His head snapped up, and he stared at me. His mouth opened and closed. A stream of emotions crossed his face. He didn't speak.

"It didn't work," I said. "Whatever stupid plan you had, it didn't work. You didn't recover stronger. You aren't going to recover at all." I paused, the words choking me. "How could you do this?"

He didn't have an answer.

I left. I didn't speak to the others in the hall. In the bedroom, I washed and changed out of my nightclothes before grabbing a cloak and heading for the stairs. I needed to be in the clear, cold air of the Frost.

FOUR

WIND BLEW THE scent of snow blossoms across my face as I ducked beneath tree branches and skirted fallen limbs. It was good to be out and moving. It helped me think.

I reached the place I sought and paused to catch my breath. Ahead, the outline of Borde's ruined lab shimmered at the edge of the forest. I shook the snow from my boots, and slipped down the hill to the hidden path that led to the front door.

The floorboards creaked with my every step as I slipped inside. I hadn't been back since we'd overthrown the Farthers and driven them from the Frost, and I didn't know what drew me back now. I walked through the rooms slowly, running my fingers over the ruined furniture and the dust-covered devices that lay forgotten and rusted now, feeling the grimy metal and aged wood and remembering the nights I'd spent there. I stopped in the center of the room and shut my eyes. Perhaps if I concentrated, I could recall everything Borde had told me about the Sickness, about the search for the cure. Had he mentioned anything offhand that might help my brother?

But I could think of nothing new.

As I stepped toward the kitchen, one of the floorboards clattered beneath the heel of my boot.

I paused.

The floorboard was warped, perhaps, or simply loose. I studied the ground below my feet. The board I'd stepped on sat a little higher than the rest of them. Maybe...?

I crouched down, gripped it with both hands, and yanked. The board came up easily, and beneath it was a narrow space stuffed with papers. A hiding place? I dipped my hand inside and shuffled through the papers. Most were unintelligible to me—diagrams, lists, other things that made little sense to me. Then my fingers brushed leather, and my heart skipped a beat. I reached deeper and withdrew a book. A journal.

My heart thudded. My throat tightened. With shaking fingers, I opened the book to the first page and saw the sign of the Thorns.

This was the journal Doctor Borde had showed me five hundred years in the past. The one that had held my family's riddle.

I turned the pages slowly. Some were filled with the scrawl of a shaking hand, unreadable passages of frantic words. Others held rows of deliberate, neat words, the shape of the letters dark from some pressing hand. I flipped faster. Here was the riddle—*What woven secret will keep you warm?* Here was the sketch of me, or someone who looked just like me. I touched the face of the girl as goose bumps rippled over my flesh.

I tucked the journal back in the space where I'd found it, replaced the board, and stood. My whole body felt wrung out, shaken. This journal, this ruin—these things were like ghosts from the past, haunting me. I didn't want them.

I stood for a moment in the stillness of the ruined lab, taking one last look around the room. Then I slipped out the door and headed for Iceliss.

~

The rustle of trees made me pause along the path to the village. The wall of vegetation parted, and a man emerged. I recognized him at once.

"Stone," I said.

The Wanderer nodded at me in greeting. "Lia Weaver."

It was strange to see him here in my world, standing among our snow blossoms and pines instead of on his wind-swept ice plain. But then again, in a way, nothing was strange anymore.

I searched for something to say, something pleasant to this once captor, now ally whose people shared the Frost with us in exchange for their assistance in overthrowing our oppressors.

"How are your people?" I finally asked. The people who called themselves the Wanderers had made a new camp near the village, close enough to trade for goods when they needed them, but far enough that we did not see each other without purposing to do so.

He considered his words before replying. "They are adjusting slowly. It is different now, to have access to this place. We are not used to seeing walls and houses of stone."

I nodded. They'd been in the village a few times, and they always moved like deer, furtive and easily startled by anything that moved too suddenly or made too loud a noise.

"We still keep our own customs," he continued. "We have pitched our tents at the far end of the Compound land, far from this place. With our ability to escape harm from the Mechs, some of us can hunt freely at night."

I nodded. We'd shared the serum that kept the Watchers—or Mechs, as Stone called them—at bay with those of the Wanderers' tribe who'd joined us in the liberation of Iceliss. It had been necessary for our plot to work, as all the people present in the village square had to be able to repel the Watchers and drive them toward the Farthers instead. It was also how we'd convinced them to help us in the first place. Now, anyone whose blood carried the serum could walk the Frost freely.

"Do you go to Iceliss now?" I asked.

Stone's expression shuttered. "Unfortunately, yes. I must obtain goods there. I bring furs to trade."

"Unfortunately?"

"We are not always welcome," he said shortly.

I remembered the conflict yesterday in the village, and the angry words aimed at "outsiders." I flinched.

"I'm sorry to hear that. You are always welcome in my house," I said.

His eyes were dark as they held mine. "And you, Lia Weaver, are always welcome in our camp. If you ever need anything, ask me."

We parted, and I headed for the former Mayor's house. Adam's new mission. Jonn's health. The letter from my mother.

I found Ivy in the bedroom when I opened the door. She sat on the bed, running her fingers over the edge of the quilt absentmindedly. I recognized it as my mother's Frost quilt, a piece cunningly woven as a map that depicted key places in our land, including Iceliss and other ancient ruins.

"I spoke to Jonn," she said, without turning around.

I let the door shut behind me. I drifted to the side of the bed but didn't sit.

"And?"

She lowered her head. Her fingers continued to stroke the quilt determinedly, as if the fabric were in need of soothing.

"He said you told him he was dying."

I sighed. I wouldn't deny it.

Ivy's face creased with anger. "He would hardly speak to me. He stared at the wall and mumbled answers. How could you upset him at a time like this?"

"Upset him? I told him the truth. He needed to know."

Ivy snorted. "Don't try to make your motives out to be so selfless and moral. You were angry with him."

"Aren't you? He did this to himself! He infected himself on purpose, Ivy, and now he's dying! He's leaving us, just like..." Like everyone else always did. But I didn't say that. It was too painful.

"He infected himself?"

"Yes! He tricked me into bringing the Sickness back in a box, and he made himself sick to try to cure his crooked leg and his seizures. And now he's dying."

My sister was silent for a long time. "He has lost all hope, Lia. I think maybe you know what that feels like."

I shook my head. "I've never done what he's done. I can't simply accept what he did and move on without feeling angry."

"Not everyone is you," she said quietly. "We don't all have your strength, your stamina." The words were an accusation, and they left me feeling tired and alone.

"I'm sorry," I said. "I've been harsh. I..." I couldn't continue the sentence, so I stopped.

Ivy reached out one hand and squeezed my fingers. There was an eloquence to her silence. Slowly, like falling asleep, I leaned my head on her shoulder. She cried, the tears dripping onto my neck, and I sat motionless and absorbed her grief as I stared at the bureau and thought about the letter inside it.

When should I tell her what I'd discovered?

Should I tell her?

At the moment, introducing more questions into my family's life was the last thing I wanted to do.

Instead of reaching for the drawer, I put both arms around Ivy. Hesitantly, I patted her back, and she gripped me with both hands and sobbed.

In the end, I didn't say anything about the letter. I didn't say anything at all.

FIVE

ADAM AND I sat before a flickering fire burning in the grate of the Mayor's parlor. Darkness swathed the house, and all the other rooms were quiet. Everyone else slept. I sat cross-legged on the ground in the middle of the rug, just close enough to the fire to feel the warmth on my face. Adam faced me, his back to the wall and his hands on his knees. He was a picture of patience, like a predator waiting in the forest for its prey. His eyes tracked my nervous hand movements, and he didn't speak as I poured out my worries and objections about his mission to Aeralis and my duties as I remained behind.

"The villagers are restless and angry. They're hearing rumors about the Sickness. They're uncertain about the Wanderers. It seems unwise for most of the agents to leave at this time. I...I just don't know if I trust the Trio's judgment in this," I finished.

Adam's expression was unreadable. "You are not required to continue serving as a Thorns operative now that the Frost has been liberated," he said. "The resulting new government—what system you have in place now—is friendly to our cause, and we have no need for secrecy here. We can work as allies with the Frost dwellers. You may be freed from your oath, if you wish."

You may be freed from your oath.

Was that what he wanted? Was that what *I* wanted?

I'd never found being a member of the Thorns oppressive. But now that our struggles here were of a different sort, perhaps it was time for me to withdraw myself. However, I still believed in their cause. I still wanted to be a part of it. I shook my head.

"I still want to help."

Adam didn't smile, but the muscles around his eyes and mouth relaxed. He'd been worried? Did he think I would part from the Thorns so easily?

"What about you?" I asked.

His eyes darkened into some emotion I couldn't read. "I cannot untangle myself so easily. Nor do I wish to. I have other objectives yet to be achieved."

"So you're going to leave." As I spoke the words, a hard lump formed in the pit of my stomach. I felt sick.

"Yes." He looked away, at the fire, and his eyelashes flickered. I couldn't tell what he thought about it.

"How can the Trio expect you to integrate into Aeralian society if you go to Astralux to aid the rebellion there?" I demanded. "Where will you stay? You have no money, no connections. What do the Thorns want from you? Magic? This is madness."

"The Thorns have operatives in Astralux," he said quietly after a while. "I am not without connections. And there are Korr and Gabe."

My heart jumped at the mention of Gabe. "I'm not sure how useful those two will be."

"I think we could come to an arrangement if necessary."

An arrangement.

"Do you trust them?"

He shrugged gracefully. He wore an unreadable expression.

"What kind of arrangement?" I asked.

"I've been thinking," he said. "We've already had at least one of our operatives spend some time in Astralux."

"You?"

He smiled faintly. "Yes, but an intimate knowledge of the walls of a prison cell is hardly useful in this instance. No, I was thinking of another operative who could accompany me and help me integrate into Aerialian society."

"*Ann?*"

He nodded.

Indignation rushed over me in a hot wave. "I don't...How could you ask her to...?" I stopped, overwhelmed by my objections. My friend had already gone through so much. She'd spent months in captivity there. And now he wanted her to return?

"Think about it," Adam said. "She has all the connections. She knows the city somewhat, she and Korr have an understanding of sorts, and she and her father were recently expelled from Iceliss."

"An understanding," I repeated. Is that what we would call it?

He tipped his head to one side, that maddening gesture that meant everything and nothing.

"And you? What are you supposed to be to her? Her brother? Her betrothed? Her servant?"

"Perhaps," he said. "We haven't arranged a story yet for me."

We sat in silence a moment. He was contemplative; I was seething. I didn't want to send Ann back into the sneering clutches of Korr.

I took a deep breath and released it slowly.

"What does Ann think?"

~

I'd expected her to refuse instantly when Adam told her his plan, or at least I'd expected her to rant at the injustice of being forced to endure Korr's presence again, but she said nothing for a long time. She sat with her hands in her lap and her head down. Her shoulders rose and fell as she breathed, and then she raised her head and looked at Adam. Her eyes gleamed like stars, hard and bright. "I'll go," she said.

"What?" I demanded.

"I'll go."

Adam nodded, relief evident in the way he flicked his eyes to mine and the way his mouth curled ever so slightly at the corners. "I will speak with the Trio."

"Perhaps you should take some time to consider—" I sputtered after he left.

"No," she said. "I'm sure."

"Ann," I said. "They can't make you do this. You've paid your debt to the Thorns. You can withdraw from the organization if you wish, and it's safe enough for you to do so and simply stay here. Adam told me about it last night. Any of us could, if we wished."

Ann stood and paced to one of the farmhouse windows. She pressed one hand to the glass. When she spoke, her breath fogged the pane. "I'm needed there, and I'm not needed here. I have no skills to aid the village during this time of transition. My quota was always a sham. I'm useless, and I'm not welcome here any longer."

"You're not useless," I said firmly. "And the Frost is your home. You are always welcome in it."

"I wish that were true. Maybe someday, if I do this, I will be."

My eyes burned. She had sacrificed so much for us, and she was being driven away. I wanted to choke just thinking about it.

Ann reached out and touched my hand. "I want to go, Lia. I need to go."

Her words did not reassure me. Instead, they filled me with dread.

~

That night, before another fire in the parlor of the former Mayor's house, Adam explained the plan to me. Ann would accompany him by wagon into the Aeralian wilderness, where they'd meet a Thorns operative called Raven at a farmhouse across the border. There, they'd trade their Frost garments and wagon for Farther fare.

I listened to everything he said without comment, and when he'd finished, I stared into the flames.

"Lia," Adam said gently. "She'll be all right."

"You'll be working with Korr."

"We've worked with him before."

I sighed. "Yes, but—"

Adam studied my face. "Is this discomfort stemming from a concern for Ann or a distaste for Korr's affection for her?"

I swallowed. I didn't have an answer.

He reached for my hand. "I won't tell you not to worry, but I will promise you that we'll be careful and vigilant."

I squeezed his fingers in thanks.

~

Adam and I walked the Frost together for what might be our final time. Icicles dripped on my cheeks, my hair. Flowers were unfolding against the melting ice. Green misted the distance. My cloak felt heavy and useless. Green growth had begun to push through the snow, and spots of color dotted the white landscape. Winter was fading.

But inside, I was a frozen block of numbness.

"After we meet the Thorns operative on the Aeralian plain, Ann will continue on alone to Korr's house in Aeralis, and I will travel into Astralux via a different route, so our arrivals do not occur simultaneously and thus do not attract any undue notice," he explained as we walked.

Visions of the too-wide Aeralian landscape, the waving grasses and the gaping sky, filled my mind and threatened to split me. I drew my imaginings back to the present and turned to him.

"Do you think anyone would be watching for your arrival?" I asked.

He paused a moment, brushing a branch away from his eyes before responding. His expression shifted as if he were remembering some long-ago incident that still caused him pain. "You'd be surprised."

Aeralis. This was really happening. Pain splintered in my chest. I dragged in a lungful of snow-scented air and let it out before speaking. "And what about those you're leaving here? What will you tell them? What should I tell them?"

"Ivy can know," he said, his eyes searching mine. "Jonn, of course. But the rest, well, they cannot know about the mission. Let them think what they want. No one will be surprised to see Ann leave, so her actions will need little explanation."

"You could pretend to move back into the Frost," I said, looking around for something to focus on besides his face so he wouldn't see the distress on mine. "Back to your farm."

"Perhaps," he said.

I drew in a string of short breaths. I would not ask him to stay again, but I ached to.

He reached out to touch me, but his hand stopped before his fingers brushed mine. "The Frost is still vulnerable. Our fledgling freedom could be dashed in an instant. We need stability. All of us. Even the Farthers. By going, I am protecting them." He lowered his voice. "I'm protecting you."

We stood there, surrounded by forest and feelings and thousands of words left unspoken, and my heart broke into a hundred pieces. When I couldn't stand it any longer, I turned and headed for the village. Adam let me go without following.

~

They left in the early dark of morning.

I joined Adam as he left the Mayor's house to retrieve Ann. Our eyes met and I sighed quietly; he nodded. Together, we descended the steps of the house and headed for the center of town. The silence between us was a world of words—he touched my hand just once, a graze of his fingers across my palm that sent tingles through my arm and to my heart, a gesture of support and affection. I stepped closer to him, and he didn't move away.

We passed through the village and reached the gate, flanked by steel reminders of our recent occupation. We entered the Cages, and the shadows still had the power to make me shudder as they flicked over my face and shoulders. I walked fast, my footsteps punctuating the hush of the Frost. Adam matched my pace without comment.

We went first to his family's farm, where a wagon waited for us. His brother, Abel, chopped wood in the yard. He stopped when he saw us and came forward. He gave me no greeting, but his eyes were friendly.

"They're harnessed and ready," he said of the horses, nodding at the wagon and the two shaggy ponies hitched to it.

"I'll make sure they're returned to you," Adam promised. Abel grunted, a sign that perhaps he put no stock in such promises, but he didn't argue.

Adam climbed into the driver's seat of the wagon. I pulled myself up next to him. One more nod passed between him and Abel, and we were off, lurching over the path toward the Weaver farm.

The wagon crested the hill of my family's farm, and my heart caught in my throat. Every time I saw it, an ache throbbed in the place below my breastbone. I missed it— fire on the hearth, a tangle of wool in my hands, a scolding for Ivy on my lips, a look exchanged between my twin and me, my parents.

Ann and her father waited in front of the farmhouse. They looked forlorn from a distance, like two dolls that had been left out in the snow by a careless child. They stood close together, but without touching. Ann held a sack of her things.

Adam stopped the wagon in the yard and climbed down from the seat to assist her. He took her sack and tossed it into the back, where Abel had spread hay to soften the wooden floor of the wagon.

I jumped into the snow and took Ann's hands. She was so pale, so fragile. She squeezed my fingers and gave me a smile that did little to reassure me.

"Are you all right?"

"As well as I've been in a long time," she promised.

Adam returned to the driver's seat, and Ann and I climbed into the back and made ourselves comfortable on the straw. I tugged my cloak over my legs and leaned my head back against the edge of the wagon. Ann's curls bounced with every lurch of the wheels, and the sight made me wish for a simpler time again, when we were merely two friends taking walks together and giggling about siblings and boys. Well, Ann had giggled about boys. I'd never been much for the subject.

"We'll be together, you know," Ann said, breaking the silence.

"What?"

"In Aeralis. Adam and I are both staying at Korr's house in the city. I'm glad of it. It'll be good to have a familiar face around this time."

"That's good," I said. The thought comforted me.

The wagon rattled as we reached the road toward Aeralis. I breathed in the smell of the Frost and saw the mountains visible through a break in the tree line. My heart ached. I did not want Adam and Ann to return to that city of fog.

I went with them as far as the river, and then Ann hugged me before I slid from the wagon bed to the snow.

Adam climbed down after me. He stood beside the horses, watching me. His cloak swirled in the wind.

I took a step forward. "Be careful," I said.

A smile tugged his lips. "I'm always careful."

I gave him a reproachful look. "You managed to get caught last time."

"Yes, but it resulted in a most spectacular rescue and a most spectacular kiss."

"Don't count on it happening again," I said, taking another step.

He tipped his head to one said, his expression turning mischievous. "The rescue or the kiss?"

"Hmm," I said.

He caught me in his arms, and I slipped my hands into his hair. "Just be careful," I murmured, and kissed him.

After a moment, he released me and stepped back. "We'll see each other soon."

I didn't answer.

He climbed up into the driver's seat. I moved away and watched as the carriage descended the bank and began to cross the black water of the river that flowed between Aeralis and the Frost. My throat squeezed. Adam didn't look back. I didn't look away.

When mist had obscured them from my view, I turned and went back to the village. I shut myself up in my room and read the bit of letter from my mother, tracing the words with my fingers and mulling their meaning in my mind. Hours passed, and I napped fitfully. When I woke, bathed in sweat and churning with the remnants of nightmares, an unsettled sensation filled my chest.

I ached for Adam and Ann, but they were gone to Aeralis. A clawing feeling filled me. I shoved myself up and went to the door.

I needed to find Ivy.

She wasn't in the village. I headed through the gate and into the Frost. She'd be with the Watchers, of course. She was always with them now.

Snow crunched beneath my boots as I ran. The wind swirled around me, tugging at my clothes. I reached the clearing above the Watcher nest and slowed. Footsteps led toward the door that led below to where the beasts slumbered during the day. Ivy, surely. I headed toward them.

A branch snapped to my left.

"There you are," a voice said.

I turned as a figure emerged from the trees. My stomach plummeted and my eyes widened as I recognized him. A man from another world, a man I thought I'd never see again.

Gordon.

SIX

GORDON SMILED WHEN he saw me, and his teeth gleamed. He was changed—his dark hair was longer, his eyes sunken. Threads hung from his clothing, which consisted of nondescript gray robes and dirty gloves. I held still as he stepped forward into the clearing. The snow whispered beneath his boots as he walked, and the sound made my skin itch with unease.

"I've been wondering how to get you alone so we could chat," he said. "And here you are. As if you came when called." He laughed, but the skin around his eyes tightened.

I didn't speak. I waited for him to reveal what he wanted, why he was here...anything.

Gordon looked past me at the landscape. "This place has become a hellhole. I rather like it. It's poetic in a tragic way. Such a bastion of learning reduced to such darkness and squalor."

"Why are you here?" I demanded. My patience was gone. I didn't fear this man. If anything, he should be afraid. It would be dark soon, and the Watchers would be out.

"There's something I need." Gordon shifted his gaze to meet mine once more. He tipped his head. "You remember our mutual friend, Meridus Borde?"

A shiver slid down my spine. I didn't reply.

"He recently crossed into your time by use of that same device you took from me once. Perhaps you've seen him."

"I haven't," I said. My heart pounded. Borde was here? Why?

"Well, that's unfortunate for us both, because I need you to get something from him for me."

"I don't see what I have to do with it." My words were calm, but my stomach was twisting. "And how did you get here?"

"I managed to follow in his wake as he passed through the gate. When we'd both arrived here, he and his companion and I had a bit of a disagreement." Borde touched a newly knit scar on his jaw and grimaced. "He attacked me and fled. I understand he headed out of the Compound area, to the south."

"I'm sorry to hear that," I said icily. My heart beat a rhythm against my ribs. "But why are you telling me this?"

"You're going to find him for me."

I crossed my arms so he wouldn't see how they trembled. I checked his hands and belt for signs of a gun. He seemed confident, too confident that I would do what he wished. "And why would I do that?"

Gordon stepped backward until his legs brushed the bushes. He bent down and yanked something from the shadows. A figure, bound and gagged. A girl.

Ivy.

My breath evaporated from my lungs. My hands shook.

"Because if you don't," Gordon said pleasantly, "she will die."

I began to shake with rage. "Perhaps you're unaware of the way our world works now. The monsters you call Mechs roam freely at night. They'll be out soon. My blood protects me, but you..." I let my sentence trail off as I raised my eyebrows.

He didn't look frightened, just amused. "Ah," he said, "but I came prepared." He withdrew a piece of metal from his robes, and I recognized the device that stopped the Watchers when I'd been in the past, in Compound time.

I pulled a knife from my belt. "What's to stop me from taking it from you right now?"

"Before you get feisty," Gordon said, "there's something else you should know." He seized Ivy by the shoulders and turned her sideways. The sleeve of her dress dangled from her arm, torn and bloodied. Ivy's eyes were wide as they met mine. She made a strangled sound through her gag.

"I've injected this girl with a marvelous invention from my time," he said. "A capsule that can crawl through the veins of the human body on its own, almost like a living thing. I won't waste your time trying to explain the particulars. I doubt you would understand. The point is, it contains the Sickness." He let go of Ivy, and she sank into the snow at his feet. He withdrew a second device from his robes and held it up. "If I activate the capsule, it will release the Sickness into her veins."

My voice came out in a breathless whisper. "You're lying."

"Ah," he said. "I thought you might be skeptical. So I got you this." He reached again into the shadows and withdrew a cage, rusted and bent. It looked as though he'd found it in a ruin. Inside the cage was a raccoon.

"I also implanted this animal," he said. "See for yourself."

He pressed a button on the device in his hand, and the raccoon twitched and shivered.

"I gave it a rather large dose, so it should begin to succumb within the day," he said. "This girl has perhaps two weeks before the capsule inside her dissolves. You don't have much time to decide you believe me."

I couldn't breathe. "Why are you doing this?"

"You know this world," he said. "I do not. I have no hope of finding Borde on my own. He has a guide, otherwise he'd be as ill equipped as I. But I have faith in you. You'll find him. You're tenacious, if nothing else."

"And if I find this device you want?"

"I'll heal her," he said. "I know the cure."

I know the cure.

The words barely registered amid the blind horror and fury swirling in my mind, but I felt the weight of them anyway.

My eyes were burning. "And if she dies before I can find this device you want?"

"I'll infect someone else." He pocketed the device and stepped back. "Find Borde and get the device he came to find." He tossed me a box. "Return to this place and light one of these when you have it, and I'll find you. Don't try to find me before you have the device; I'll detonate the capsule."

With that, he vanished into the trees.

I ran to Ivy and fell to my knees beside her. My fingers scraped at the knots binding her wrists. I yanked the gag from her mouth. She struggled up as her bonds fell off, and I caught her before she could slump forward. She shook beneath my hands. I cradled her against my chest, and she hid her face against my neck.

"He came out of nowhere," she said, her voice muffled. "He hit me over the head and injected that thing. When I awoke, he'd already bound and gagged me."

I squeezed her close. She was warm from crying. She squeaked as I bumped her injured arm, and I relaxed my hold, but only slightly.

"Did he know you were my sister?" I asked.

She shook her head. "He said something about watching me make trips into the forest often. None of the other villagers venture into the Frost much, except

Trappers and Fishers, and they must have been too large for him to want to attack."

I helped her to her feet. "Let's get you back to the village. The Healers will examine you. He might be insane, or bluffing." Hope was just a prickle at the edge of my panic.

"Wait, the raccoon," she said, stopping to look for the cage. "We should bring it." Her face softened at the sight of the shivering animal huddled in the corner of his cage, and my chest twisted with pain. Ivy, the ever-compassionate one. Protector of injured raccoons and risker of her own self.

"Let's go," I said.

~

The Healers tended to Ivy and examined the raccoon while I paced a path in the floor outside. Clocks ticked. The sunlight coming through the windows slowly slid across the hall. My heart slammed against my ribs hard and fast like a fist beating on a door, demanding answers.

Finally, one of the Healers emerged from the room where they'd taken my sister. Her mouth was pressed in a flat line, and her eyes slid past mine to the floor as she spoke.

"We believe she is indeed in danger of being infected. The raccoon is already showing signs of the disease."

My blood burned and white spots danced across my vision. I went to my room and shut the door.

I had to find Borde and retrieve this thing Gordon wanted. There was no other alternative. But where would I even start? I was all alone in this, and there wasn't much time.

Dropping my head into my hands, I inhaled deeply and let my thoughts clear. I could do this. I just needed to *think*.

The tickle of a memory filled my mind. Stone, telling me a story.

"And yet you've heard of Weavers?"

"There was a man," he said. "He told us about you."

"A man?"

"Yes. He came to us heavily wounded, accompanied by a companion. He was sick. He rambled in his sleep, talking of Weavers and the monsters and blood. Some of my people thought he was a prophet."

"And you?" My heart beat fast. Who was this man who spoke of my family?

"He was just a man," Stone said. "A man with knowledge."

"And his name?"

"He didn't give one. He didn't stay with us long. We called him Scar, for he had many after he'd healed."

A man, heavily wounded, accompanied by a companion, talking of Weavers and monsters and blood.

I needed to speak to Stone.

~

I slowed as I reached the center of the village on my way to the Frost, spotting a crowd gathered in front of the Assembly Hall. I heard mutters on the wind and sensed a brewing ugliness on the air, but my mission tugged at me heavily, and I didn't stop.

I would tend to their arguments later.

The snow crunched beneath my boots as I left the village. Snow blossoms spilled across the paths in waving stalks of blue, and the trees hung over the path, heavy with new verdure. Above the screams of the bluewings, I heard the rushing of new streams that threaded between tree trunks and around icy stones. The world was shrieking and seeping and dripping. The Frost was restless. It matched the pace of my heartbeat.

The Wanderers' camp was several miles beyond my family's farmstead. The tents cropped up abruptly from the forest floor like a cluster of boulders. A branch snapped beneath me as I approached, and guards materialized from behind trees. Their eyes searched my face, and they lowered their weapons.

"I'm looking for Stone," I said, in a tone that signaled I was not someone to be trifled with, not today. My entire world was collapsing around me. I was iron and fire inside.

One of the guards melted away into the trees. The others regarded me without speaking. I stared coolly back.

After a moment, they averted their eyes.

Stone appeared at the edge of the camp. "Lia Weaver. What brings you to us?"

"We need to talk," I said.

Stone nodded to the guards, and they returned to their posts, leaving us alone. He stretched out an arm toward the paths to indicate that we should walk. I joined him.

"And how is your brother?" he asked.

"Not good," I said. "The Healers say he is dying."

"I'm sorry to hear that."

"There's more. Much more." I recounted my meeting with Gordon and the report the Healers had given me. "This must remain between us," I finished. "I can't cause a panic in the village."

"It will not leave my lips," he promised.

"Stone, do you remember when your people kidnapped me and brought me to your camp, and I asked how you knew about the power of my blood?"

He nodded. "I remember."

"You mentioned a man. You said your people called him Scar."

"Yes," Stone said.

"Tell me more about him."

"There isn't much to tell," he said. "We came across him in the woods. He was injured and sick. We sheltered him until he'd healed, and then he left us."

"You mentioned a companion who was with him?"

Stone inclined his head. "Yes, the man we called Scar was accompanied by a younger man with brown hair and sad eyes. He didn't speak much. He seemed to know the land much better than his friend."

"What happened to them?"

"I don't know," Stone said. "They headed for Aeralis."

Aeralis.

My stomach twisted. So vast and so far a place. How would I ever find him?

"They didn't say what they were looking for, or why, but they were seeking something. We did not probe." He hesitated. "He mentioned the capital city, Astralux."

I thanked Stone and headed back into the Frost. I needed to think.

The world was white and blue around me. Stingweed snagged my cloak, and I freed the hem with automatic movements as my mind spun with thoughts. Far away, I saw a mothkat flap from the rotted end of a fallen tree. The sight of the carnivorous scavenger made me think of my sister—Ivy had once rescued a wounded mothkat, something only she would do—and I bit back a sob.

What was I going to do?

Darkness began to creep across the snow. I kept walking, my steps relentless and methodical as I paced the paths of the forest. Snow blossoms brushed at my ankles. Somewhere far away, I heard the snarl of a snow panther.

Wind tossed my hair and bit my cheeks, and I smelled smoke.

I stopped. Smoke?

Unconsciously, I'd headed to my family's farm. I crept forward and broke through the wall of trees into the clearing.

The farm was burning.

Orange flames licked at the sides of the buildings and swirled up toward the sky. The roar of it filled my ears as the heat seared my face. I screamed, wept, and threw snow helplessly at the conflagration.

It was no use.

The house was almost consumed. The barn was a snarling ball of fire and soot.

The former Mayor crept from the woods to meet me. "They came," he said. "They set it on fire...I fled out a window...."

I stared into the flames. My body was numb. The blood in my veins was like ice despite the heat roasting my skin. "They?"

"People from the village," he said. "They wore masks. I didn't see their faces."

I shut my eyes. I couldn't breathe.

"I'm going to Aeralis," Ann's father said. "I cannot stay here."

"No," I agreed. "You should go at once."

Without another word, I turned and headed for the village.

~

I flung open the door to the Assembly Hall. The sound of the knob hitting the wall reverberated through the space. Heads turned. Someone stood at the front of the room speaking. A Fisher. He paused to stare at me.

I stalked down the aisle. My clothes were sooty. My skin was blistered from the heat of the fire. My hands were clenched.

"What are you—" he began.

"Shut up," I roared.

He shut up.

I reached the front and whirled to face the room. They were here, half the village, sitting with their hands folded and their mouths shut, looking at me in confusion and bewilderment. Some of them frowned knowingly.

"What is wrong with you?" I demanded.

Silence.

"You burned my farm. You. Burned. My. Farm."

The Fisher tried to speak. I cut him off.

"If you cannot stop this madness, we are all going to kill each other. We have to work together. We are free from the Farthers, but we are not free from our own fear!"

They were all very still.

"You will rebuild my family's farm," I snarled. "You'll do it when I get back."

"Get back?" someone ventured.

I left without answering.

~

I paced in my room in the house on the hill until Ivy found me. She sagged in the doorway, hair disheveled, clothing still torn and stained with her blood, face white.

"They burned the farm," I said tonelessly. "I don't know who did it. Villagers. Idiots. I think all of our things—Ma's quilts, Da's notebooks, all of it—are gone." I looked at her. If I didn't do something, she would be gone soon, too.

Ivy sat on the bed. Her skin was the color of bleached bone.

"What are we going to do?" she asked.

"Earlier, I spoke to Stone. He told me a few months ago about a man they'd helped, a man who'd known who I was. I think it might have been Borde."

"Oh," she said.

"But there's a problem. Stone says Borde left for Aeralis. Astralux, maybe."

Gabe's words floated into my mind. *If you ever need anything, if you ever are in Aeralis and you need to find me, come to the Plaza of Horses.*

"Oh," Ivy said again. "And?"

Resolution hardened in my gut. "I'm going to find him. I'm going to Aeralis."

Ivy chewed her lip. She looked at me, and her eyes shimmered with apprehension and hope. "That man said I have a few weeks before I'm infected. Do you think it will be enough time?"

I didn't answer, because I didn't know.

SEVEN

I PACKED THE next morning before the sun had risen. One sack, filled with the plainest garments I could find.

"Most of our clothing won't be any good in Aeralis," I'd overheard Adam explaining to Ann days ago before they'd left. "We'll get new clothes," he'd told her. "So take only what you'll need for the journey."

I had no such luxury awaiting me, so I selected the things that would blend best with the fashions I remembered from my last trip. I brushed my fingertips over the folded garments I was leaving behind. I was not sentimental, but something tethered me to the moment, holding me in place long enough to remember the things I'd done while wearing this cloak, that dress, those shoes.

Ivy was below in the foyer of the Mayor's house, her eyes wide and her mouth stiff against any signs of telltale emotion when she spotted me with my bag, ready to leave. She looked older than the image of her I carried in my heart as she rose and watched me descend the stairs. She smoothed both hands down her dress and lifted her shoulders like a bird about to take flight. She was hope embodied. She was an angel. She was my sister, so precious and fragile. I ached at the thought of leaving her.

"I won't be able to write," I said. It was a stupid thing to say, but an unexpected rush of emotion flooded my head and muddled my thoughts.

"Of course not," Ivy said, and she laughed nervously. "I won't expect letters." She stared at my face hard. "The Thorns—?"

"What about them?"

She twisted her fingers together. "Do they know you're coming to Aeralis? I thought you were supposed to stay here."

"Hang the Thorns if they think I'll sit by idly and watch you die," I snapped, although a flicker of fear ran through me at her question. I didn't have time to wonder about that now, though.

I looked back at the stairs, thinking of the barely-breathing young man that slept in the sickroom. "Take care of Jonn for me."

"You should say goodbye," Ivy said.

A tug-of-war pulled my heart in two directions, but in the end, I heeded her suggestion and climbed the stairs again, alone, to get one last glimpse. When I reached his room, the Healer said I could go in, even though he was sleeping again and might not wake. I slipped inside and approached his bed. His eyes were shut, and his chest rose and fell beneath the quilt. I reached for his hand but didn't touch him.

"I'm going away," I whispered. "Something's happened. Ivy will get the Sickness if I don't." I chewed my lip until blood flowed over my tongue as I stared at a hole in the quilt. "If you hadn't done this to yourself, I wouldn't be alone," I said.

He didn't move.

"They burned the farm, Jonn," I said.

Jonn stirred but didn't wake.

Maybe it was better that Da's journals were gone, if that was what had led to Jonn's idea for giving himself the Sickness in the first place. Anger rose in me, squeezing my throat shut. I rose and left the room.

Ivy waited by the door, the courage in her eyes threadbare and her smile tremulous. My heart was a stone in my chest as I looked at her.

"I'll come back to you," I promised. "I'll find Borde and that device. I'll fix this, Ivy."

"Lia..." She faltered. "But if you don't... I mean..."

"I'll come back," I said firmly. "I always have before." I hugged her, and she was brittle in my arms—bony, restless with hope and sadness, bristling with bravado. I savored the warmth of her breath against my cheek, the tickle of her hair on my hands, and her scent of wool and charcoal and snow blossoms. She smelled like our home.

We stepped away from each other. I could delay no longer, not if I wanted to get a good start on the journey today. I went to the door and opened it without looking back, but I sensed her eyes on me all the way to the porch and into the yard.

I passed beneath the bars of the Cages into the Frost as dawn broke through the trees. The path was empty, and I ran it, just like in the days when I'd been rushing to deliver quota on time. My breath escaped from my lips in puffs of white, and my heartbeat kept time with my pounding footfalls. Around me, the white wilderness trembled with uneasy silence.

By the time my sides were aching and my legs were trembling from the run, I reached the river that separated the Frost from Aerialian land. My steps slowed. I stopped and stared at the rushing black water, and memories fell over me like a mist. I had a flash of a recollection of Cole at my elbow as we lingered at the brink of this river, catching sight of Aerialian soldiers through the trees. That had been before everything had started. Before everything had changed. When he was just a young village boy who wanted to court me, and I didn't know he'd murdered my parents. I didn't know what my Weaver blood meant. I didn't know how much my heart could love.

Back then, nobody dared to cross the river.

Sucking in a deep breath, I gathered my courage and stepped into the icy water. Froth swirled around the soles of my boots as I leaped from rock to rock, avoiding the deepest parts. I reached the other side, and as I scrambled up the muddy bank, my stomach plummeted. I'd officially crossed into Aeralis.

There was no turning back now.

Mist clung to the trees on this side of the river, obscuring everything but the ground right in front of me. Light lanced through the gray, and then I was breaking through the fog as I reached level ground and left the river behind. An endless sky piled with clouds and a field of broken stalks and half-melted snow stretched away for miles. There were no trees. A cold wind swept over me and made my cloak curl around me.

This was Aeralis.

I'd seen it before when Korr and I had jumped a train and traveled to Astralux to rescue Adam, but that time, the world had whirled past in a blur. Now it stretched before me, unbroken and vast, a plain of dirty brown grass and a blank gray sky.

I began walking.

The whole day passed without any change in the landscape, until finally, as the sun was sinking, a dot appeared at the place where the fields met the sky. As I grew closer, a house took shape. Straggling fence posts formed a paddock to the left, and a lone barn huddled to the right. A single light glowed in an upper window.

I stopped in a yard of packed earth. The farmhouse was large, built of thick gray timbers. The barn behind it was built of sod. I approached the house and rapped the knocker twice, with three beats of silence in between. A Thorns signal.

Footsteps rang out on the other side, and the hinges groaned as someone cracked the door and peered out.

Brilliant honey-brown eyes gazed at me, and the crack widened to reveal a young woman with thick black hair and a constellation of freckles one shade darker than her tanned skin. She was young, perhaps my age, but when she frowned at me, her mouth had a curve of perception that made her look much older. She sized me up with a glance of disinterest.

"Can I help you?"

I traced the sign of the Thorns in the dirt at my feet. A twinge of guilt filled me—my orders had been to remain in the Frost, and I was misusing information meant for other agents that I shouldn't know in the first place—but it was only a twinge. I needed her help, and this was the only way she'd trust me.

"Ah," the girl said. "I see. And your name?"

I straightened. "Bluewing.

The girl's eyes widened slightly, and her cynical smile faded. I felt the slightest nudge of pleasure that I'd managed to impress her.

"I've heard of your triumph in the Frost," she said, and stepped aside to let me in.

"Are you Raven?" I asked.

She smirked at the question. "My ma and da named me Nettie, but I won't answer to it, so don't bother. Besides, Raven is a much more appropriate description, don't you think?" She flipped her dark locks and turned to shut the door behind us.

The interior of the house was lit only by smoking kerosene lamps fastened to the walls. Farming equipment hung on hooks, and animal skins crowded the wood-planked walls. Old feed sacks were tacked into place in the empty place, and rusted firearms were mounted over a stone fireplace filled with smoldering coals. A haphazard stack of books dominated the corners of the room, and one stack replaced the fourth leg of a table beneath a window. The floorboards creaked beneath our boots.

"What is this place?" I asked.

"It's an inn," Raven said, clicking her tongue against her teeth as if disapproving of my inability to deduce that fact from the jumble of incomprehensible objects. She gestured around us. "These things are just for decoration. The visitors from the city like it. Makes it seem rustic. We keep the real goods in the barn."

I wandered close to the fireplace. One of the guns looked like the one that had belonged to my father. I reached out a hand.

"Careful," she said. "Those are real. I like to keep them close in case soldiers come calling."

I pulled my hand back.

"I wasn't expecting another operative," she said.

Another. Of course. Adam and Ann had passed through here only days ago.

"I'm bound for Astralux," I said. "But I'll need directions. I don't know the way."

"Of course," she said. "I can get you a map. A horse, too."

"Thank you."

"I'm a Thorns operative," Raven said. "It's my job." She murmured something about seeing to my room and headed for the stairs.

Loneliness tore through me as I stood alone in the dim room and thought of my family, my home. I was lost without that bright blue sky and white, wild world.

The stairs squeaked, and Raven appeared again at the top of them.

"Better come up now," she said. "I don't want my parents to hear and get curious. They're old and keep to their room mostly, but they aren't deaf. They don't know about my, er, additional loyalties. I'll bring you dinner in your room."

I ascended the stairs, and she showed me to a cubbyhole of a room set beneath the rafters of the house. I tumbled into the rickety bed and shut my eyes, listening to the wail of the wind around the eaves of the house as I tried to calm myself. Raven returned after a short while, carrying a tray of dense bread and a bowl of thick, congealed stew that was mostly beets and carrots with a few slivers of meat. It seemed the Frost wasn't the only place that had experienced lean years lately.

"We'll leave in the morning," she said.

"We?"

"I have a feeling you're going to get lost on your own."

I bristled at her implication that I wasn't capable of finding Astralux by myself.

Raven laughed. "Relax, Frostie. I have business in Astralux myself, and I don't see why we shouldn't go together. Like I said, we'll leave in the morning."

After she left, I ate the food slowly. It was coarse but filling. When I'd finished, I lay down on the narrow bed. Exhaustion pulled at my limbs and eyelids, but my mind was restless and my blood warm with worry. When dreams came, they were filled with the Frost, and I woke with a whisper of foreboding on my lips.

I dressed in the dark and fumbled for my things. Voices sounded downstairs, and I opened the door. But when I stepped into the hall, I stopped at the harsh tenor of the words below. Sweat prickled across my back, and my heart slammed in my chest as I peeked around the corner.

Farther soldiers.

EIGHT

RAVEN'S VOICE MATCHED the soldiers' in intensity.

"I have no idea what you're talking about," she insisted.

I pressed my back to the wall and inched forward to peer over the railing. Below, three gray-coated soldiers stood in the doorway, guns in their hands and scowls on their faces. Pale morning light spilled around them, illuminating part of the room and turning Raven's face a luminescent white. She'd drawn a wool cloak around her shoulders, and her dark hair hung in disheveled waves down her back. She seemed younger, vulnerable. When she spoke again, her tone was pleading.

"You'll wake my da," she said in a wheedling tone. "He'll be angry."

"If I find spies in this house, your da will rot in His Excellency's prison. That should worry him more than his lack of sleep."

"Look if you wish," she said. "You'll find nothing, I swear it. Go on, search all the rooms!"

The soldier gazed at her face as if he could peel off her skin with the sheer force of his stare. She returned it, her expression equal parts defiance and fright. The soldier sniffed once in derision. He signaled to the others with a snap of his gloved hand, turned on his heel, and left.

I exhaled in relief.

Raven's shoulders sagged as the soldiers slammed the door behind them. She pressed one hand to her forehead and sank into a nearby chair. I heard her mutter something under her breath, and her hands trembled as she pulled the cloak tighter around her shoulders.

I stepped to the stairs, and they creaked with my weight. Raven turned as she heard me, and her expression smoothed as easily as butter across a roll. A smirk that was rapidly becoming familiar quirked on her lips as she looked up at me.

"Did the soldiers wake you? They have a knack for that. It must be one of the requirements for recruitment."

"Were they looking for Thorns operatives?" I asked.

She snorted. "They don't have the foresight for that. No, they were looking for Restorationists. There are rumors of them passing through this area lately—rumors planted by us, of course, to give them something to fret about. The soldiers have been combing every nook and cranny searching for them."

Restorationists. I remembered Gabe mentioning the term. He was one of them now.

"Breakfast?" Raven said, flipping her hair over her shoulder and sauntering toward the fireplace with a swish of her hips. "I feel like breaking something. Let's have eggs."

~

I waited alone in the barn after we'd eaten. Raven joined me half an hour later, carrying a sack of her things.

"Shall we?" she asked, as if we were going out for a pleasure ride.

We rode out on two shaggy ponies with black and white patches. The sky was the color of dirty water. Wind whipped our hair and dragged at our cloaks. My mount snorted, lifting his nose toward the paddock. I steered him to the road, and he reluctantly picked up his feet and headed toward the horizon.

"He smells a storm," Raven said, clucking to her pony under her breath.

I glanced at the clouds, and apprehension brewed in my stomach. "A blizzard?"

"We don't get too much snow here," she said. "The winds come from the south, and they're warmer than in your Frost."

That was a mercy, since we had a ways to go before we reached the city, but part of me ached to see a blanket of fresh white on this broken ground of churned grass and melting sludge. A crisp fall of snow could make even the cruelest visage look soft and beautiful, and there was something about the blinding blankness that centered me and helped me think.

"We should reach Astralux tomorrow before nightfall," Raven said, breaking the silence.

I nodded calmly, but my heart thumped against my ribs and my palms tickled restlessly. I ground my teeth together and resisted the urge to fidget, instead staring straight ahead at the place where the sky and ground blurred together.

We were silent for hours, listening to the clop of the ponies' hooves. Raven whistled tunelessly under her breath. I wrestled with thoughts of Jonn and Ivy.

When the sun began to sink below the horizon, we dismounted to eat and build a fire. Raven produced bedrolls lined with fur, and we slept by the fire.

I woke with frost on my lashes. My muscles were stiff, and my mouth tasted like ash.

Raven handed me a piece of dried meat. "We'll eat on the road," she said. "Let's get going."

The landscape slipped past as we rode. Raven said little, but she watched me out of the corner of her eye. She hummed songs beneath her breath.

Finally, a glimmer of black appeared on the far horizon. Astralux? Fear choked me, but I swallowed it back. I was a Weaver. I had faced the gate, I had faced Watchers, and I had faced Farther soldiers. I would not let this city frighten me. I'd been here before. I would not tremble and cower.

"Astralux," Raven said, confirming what I'd seen.

As we drew closer, I could see the towers rising from the mist that clothed the city. Sunlight glittered on glass and intricate metal. A river encircled the city like a snake, its water shining like scales.

"We'll meet a Thorns agent within the city," Raven explained. She tossed her hair out of her eyes and flashed me a challenging smile as she nodded at the towers and bridges ahead of us. "It's astonishing, isn't it? Quite a change from your wilderness Frost, yes?"

"You'd be surprised what we have in the Frost," I answered, thinking of Echlos, and she shrugged.

The ponies' hooves clopped loudly as we crossed a bridge of stone so tall I had to crane my neck to see the top of it. Statues of men holding guns and swords crowned the pinnacle. A shiver went through me.

A throng enclosed us as we entered the city. Men and women clothed in thick coats and hats swarmed the streets around us, and wagons and steamcoaches rumbled past, causing my pony to shy to the left. Steam filled the air and made the ends of my hair and cloak damp. We crossed another bridge and passed down a maze of cobbled streets. Houses and businesses huddled together, hanging over the streets as if about to collapse onto them. Ropes crisscrossed the sky above us, strung with drying laundry or lanterns or fluttering banners advertising shops. The air smelled of sewage and wet flowers and horsehair. Rain began to fall, and the people in the street scurried for the overhanging buildings as we pressed on.

Raven led me into an alley, and we dismounted. A figure in a black coat stepped from a shadow and took our mounts' reins. A woman. She lifted a sputtering lantern high to dispel the gloom brought on by the rain and darkness of the alley as she peered at us suspiciously.

"Do you have business here?"

"We're meeting an uncle," Raven said, and the woman's eyebrows quirked in recognition. It must be a code.

"And how was the weather on the Aeralian plain?" she asked.

Raven licked her lip and smiled her enigmatic smirk. "We saw no lightning."

The woman nodded, satisfied. "And the sign?"

Raven flashed a Thorns brooch at her, and the woman gestured toward a door in the wall.

"You'll find food in there, as well as clothing," the woman said.

We went inside.

Gaslights glowed along the far wall, and a chandelier strung with cobwebs hung low over a table laid out with bread, cheese, and a pitcher of drink. A pile of clothing sat on a chair beside the table.

"What was that all about?" I asked.

"It's a code. Thorns operatives in the city are always meeting an uncle, and if we've seen no lightning, that means we were not followed. Then we're free to show the brooch."

Raven grabbed a piece of cheese with her fingers and stuffed it in her mouth while I surveyed the room more closely. Bookshelves surrounded a pair of shuttered windows. One of the titles caught my eye. *The Winter Parables.*

Shivers spidered over my skin.

I reached for the pile of clothes. Some were made of silks, velvets. I dug through them until I'd found something plain and sensible. Raven nodded toward a curtain, her mouth full of food.

"I think we are supposed to dress in there."

I went first, peeling off my woolen cloak and dress and putting on the black cotton trousers and shirt that had been provided. The shirt tied in the back, corset-like, cinching my waist in, and the tightness on my stomach felt strange. I put on the coat next, a long gray piece studded with brass buttons. A high collar scratched against my neck and caught my braid. I tugged at the cuffs and brushed away lint, acquainting myself with the new and strange material.

I put my discarded clothing in the sack of things I'd brought. After a moment's hesitation, I reached into the sack and found my mother's letter. I'd brought it with me. I tucked the folded paper into my belt and stepped out from behind the curtain.

Raven sized me up, and her mouth pinched with concentration. "You look Aeralian enough, but wear your hair up."

I reached back and twisted my braid into a knot.

She nodded, satisfied.

I ate a little bread and cheese while she took her turn behind the curtain. When she emerged, she wore a long gray coat over a wine-colored pair of loose trousers and a ruffled blouse. Gray silk gloves covered her hands, and she'd pulled up her hair in a thick, glossy bun at the nape of her neck. She looked utterly different.

"Well?" she asked, twirling.

I didn't say anything.

Raven grinned at me. She sauntered back to the table, plucked a piece of fruit from the platter, and then reached for the pile of clothing again with the other hand. "Perhaps

I should have chosen this shirt," she mused, holding up a silken blouse to the light.

I ignored her, already thinking ahead to what I must do next. I had no idea how I was going to find Borde. I remembered Gabe's promise. Could he possibly help me? I didn't dare try to find Adam. He'd be furious that I was here.

Raven strolled back behind the curtain with the silk shirt in her hand. "I'm going to slip this on and see if I like it better," she called.

The door behind me opened and shut with a slam, letting in a rush of wind and the sound of rain. I turned to look as a figure stepped into the room and took off a dripping hat.

I froze in utter astonishment.

Adam.

NINE

ADAM SCANNED THE room and spotted me. He went still, his shoulders tensing, his eyebrows pulling together as he regarded me. "Lia?" he spoke as if to himself only, as if I were a dream conjured in his mind.

I met his eyes without flinching, although a jolt of something electric and frightening shot through me at the intensity in his gaze. "Yes."

"What are you doing here?" The words were calm, soft, but an undercurrent of something cold lurked in them.

Raven stepped from behind the curtain in the silk shirt, and her lips curved in a slight smile as she saw Adam. "Brewer," she said, not sounding surprised. "I thought I saw Merrick slipping away through the crowd when we arrived. He must have told you right away."

Adam and Raven knew each other? Of course they did. She'd been his and Ann's contact on their way to Astralux.

Adam didn't answer her. His eyes never left mine as he laid his hat on the table and stripped off his gloves.

"Is it Jonn?" His tone was flat, with no discernible glimmer of emotion in it.

"Jonn's condition hasn't changed," I said.

Raven looked from Adam to me. We continued to ignore her. Adam raised his eyebrows at me and tipped his head. He looked calm, but I saw the tension in his fingers, his neck. His question was clear.

Why had I defied my orders?

"I'm here on a personal mission," I said.

"Personal mission?" he repeated sharply.

I looked at Raven and back at Adam. "Can we speak somewhere privately?"

Adam indicated a door in the wall, and I followed him into a paneled study lined with diamond pane windows. Pale light slanted through them, illuminating a desk strewn with books and papers.

Adam shut the door and leaned against the desk. "Tell me."

I went to the window. Where to start?

"There's a man in the Frost, a man from the old time of the Compound. He kidnapped Ivy and implanted her with some kind of capsule containing the Sickness. He wants a device that Borde is here to find, he said, and he wants me to find it. If I don't do as he says, she's going to be infected just like Jonn."

Adam stared at me as he absorbed this bizarre information without a flicker of expression. "Explain."

Explaining made me impossibly tired, but I tried. "I have to find Borde. I have to get this device from him to save my sister. Gordon says he knows the cure, and if I bring him this device—"

"Lia," Adam interrupted. "This is insane. Where is this man now?"

"I don't know. He gave me a way to contact him once I have the device."

"We should find him immediately, capture him, and force him to remove the capsule in Ivy's arm—"

"No! If we do that, he'll activate the capsule and infect her immediately. There isn't time to try to come up with some grand plan. I just have to do this, and quickly. Ivy has maybe two weeks before the capsule dissolves on its own."

"You think it will be so easy, finding Borde?"

"I think I'm not going to stand by and let my sister die!" My voice cracked with emotion, and I paused, collecting myself. "Stone told me about a man they gave shelter to only a few months ago, a man who rambled in his sleep about Weavers and blood and monsters. They called him Scar, because he came to them wounded. Adam, I believe that man was Borde."

"But how could Borde have even known our location in time in relation to his to be able to calculate his arrival?"

"I don't know, but he's here. Gordon followed him. And if I can find him..." I stopped as my throat tightened. "I know it's a risk," I continued. "But it's a risk I'm willing to take. A risk I have to take."

Adam lowered his head. "You've failed to consider one thing," he said. "Your orders. I understand why you're doing what you're doing, but the Trio—"

"I didn't fail to consider my orders."

He stiffened. "So you've deliberately defied them."

I didn't reply.

"People's lives are at stake, Lia. You can't simply leave your post and throw yourself into a mission like this. You could expose a Thorns operative, draw attention to the Restorationists, get someone killed—"

"If I don't do something, people will be killed. My family."

He didn't reply. His jaw tightened as he turned his head toward the window.

"Everything is falling apart. They burned my family's farm—"

Adam turned around so sharply that I was startled into silence.

"Who burned what?" His voice was laced with venom.

"Villagers," I said. "They set fire to it, I presume because we were allowing Ann's father to live there. Ann's father fled to Aeralis after it happened. I—"

"Iceliss is utter chaos, and you've left Ivy, Jonn, and the rest of them to come here?"

"If I didn't come, my sister would die!"

"You don't know what would happen. Gordon could be lying. Ivy might weather the Sickness on her own. With you gone, lives are at risk. Many, many lives."

My fingers formed fists at my sides as words clotted on my tongue. "You said before that I could withdraw from the Thorns if I wanted to." I spoke the words softly, but they shouted in the silence.

Adam stilled. "Yes."

"Well." I couldn't breathe. Every muscle in my body screamed with tension. "I want to withdraw."

He stared at me. "Is that your final decision?" He asked it softly, so softly I barely heard him.

"It is."

Adam's fingers tapped his leg. The slightest note of distress touched his voice. "If you do that, you will have to leave this place—it's a Thorns refuge, and you will not be authorized—"

"Then I'll leave it."

"You'll be alone in the city. It won't be safe. I won't be able to make sure you stay safe. I won't be allowed to."

"I don't need you to protect me, Brewer," I said coldly.

He flinched at my use of his last name. It was like a slap.

I handed over the Thorns brooch that I always carried, the one that had belonged to my parents, and I left.

~

Rain soaked my hair and streamed in rivulets down my coat as I crossed the street, heading deeper into the city. My legs trembled. My heart pounded along with the rain slamming against the sidewalk ahead of me.

I was on my own now.

Pain splintered in my chest, but I pushed it away. I needed to find Gabe. I needed to find the Plaza of Horses.

People hurried past, their coat collars turned up against the wet and their heads down to shield their faces from rain splatter. A steamcoach rushed past, drenching me. I gasped as icy water hit my legs, shocking me with sudden coldness.

Wiping water from my brow, I ducked into a side street. A dangling sign advertised fresh bread above a door in the wall. I opened it and went in.

The shop smelled like cinnamon and flour. Rain pattered against a stained glass window that looked over the street. Green paneled walls were filled with glass cases of flour, sugar, and grain, and baked goods filled a glass display case before a counter. Behind it, a man in a striped apron hefted a bag with a grunt and a puff of flour. He didn't look up as I approached.

"Excuse me," I said. "Can you give me directions? I'm looking for the Plaza of Horses."

The man grunted. "It's a far walk from here. Six blocks straight and take a right. It's past the river, near the Prison Sector.

"Thank you."

I was reluctant to leave that warm, sweet-smelling shop, but I had to find Gabe before nightfall. I turned up my coat collar and ventured back out into the deluge.

Darkness was beginning to fall by the time I reached the turn the baker had described. I headed right, crossing the river on a narrow metal bridge that ran parallel to the stone one for wagons. The waves beneath the bridge danced in the wind, pebbled with rain. I walked faster as I stepped off the bridge and into a different area of the city.

The walls here were higher, grayer. Many were topped with snarls of wire. The Prison Sector? I scanned the streets. Fewer pedestrians walked these sidewalks, and those who did moved furtively. At the corner, a pair of soldiers in gray uniforms stood smoking and talking. The light of their cigs glowed in the gloom. They looked at me as I passed; their gazes were lazy and appraising. I pulled my coat tighter and pressed on.

A wall lined with statues rose from the gloom of rain ahead of me. Horses. They were frozen in midstride, their mouths open, their heads tossed back, and their manes flowing. The mist parted around the wall. I saw a gate, and beyond it lay a vast space paved with flagstones.

The Plaza of Horses.

I stepped through the gate and into the square. Water splashed around my ankles as I crossed the expanse. Thunder growled above the city. A streak of lightning split the sky, filling the plaza with white light and throwing the statues into garish relief. Against the wall, a figure in a long dark coat leaned, arms crossed.

Gabe?

I started toward this unknown person, my heart hammering with hope, but when I reached him, he looked at me with blank eyes. His mouth turned down in a snarl, and he stepped away from me and lit a cig.

Not Gabe.

I moved away from him, following the wall topped with horses. Rain dripped down my face and soaked into the place where my collar rubbed against my neck. I stopped and turned a full circle, scanning the plaza. Only a few people were out in this downpour, scuttling for shelter as I watched. The rain fell so hard that fog rose off the ground. Distantly, the rumble of a wagon echoed in the street.

Despair threatened to close my throat. What was I going to do? I needed to find that statue of the stallion, but how long would I have to wait before Gabe came to check for a message?

The flutter of fabric snagged my attention, and I turned in time to see a man disappearing around the edge of the gate. For a moment, my heart leaped. Adam? It had looked like him, but whoever it was, he or she was gone.

A hand touched my shoulder, and I spun. Arms enfolded me before I could see the face of the person before me. I stiffened in surprise.

"Lia," a voice breathed in my ear, and I relaxed as I recognized that voice and remembered the shape of the arms and chest that accompanied it.

Gabe.

TEN

"GABE?" MY VOICE came out small with hope.

"What are you doing here?" He pulled back and studied my face. "I mean, it's good to see you. But what...?" His eyes scanned mine. "Are you all right?"

"It's a long story," I said. Rain splattered against my cheeks and made me blink. "But I've been better."

"Let's get out of here and get you someplace dry and warm, with something hot to drink."

That sounded wonderful. I nodded.

He let his hand slide down my arm to clasp my hand. "This way."

We crossed the plaza together, heading for one of the corners instead of the gate I'd come through. I opened my mouth to ask if he planned to walk straight through the wall, but then we were ducking through a break in the stones I hadn't noticed before. The roar of rain was muffled, replaced by dripping and splashing as water streamed down the walls of the alley around us. Gabe released my hand, because it was too narrow for us to walk side by side. I followed him up a flight of narrow stairs and through a maze of tunnels.

"Where are we?" My voice whispered around us in a faint echo.

"On the edge of the Prison Sector," Gabe explained over his shoulder. "It's full of old factories that have been converted into living spaces by the, er, less fortunate. These tunnels lead practically everywhere in this sector, and the soldiers never venture into them. They're a death trap if you're the wrong person. We use them to cross this portion of the city without detection."

Our feet rang on the stone steps as we climbed higher. Stained walls fell away to reveal rooftops. In the distance, the towers of the city looked like a cluster of needles. Below, I saw prison wagons crawling past in the streets. Horses strung with chains shook their manes in the rain, spraying water. A man shouted at a dog tugging on his pant leg. On the corner of the street, two soldiers smoked and did nothing.

Gabe stopped beside a crumbled section of wall that opened into a courtyard with a patch of gray open sky above it. Rain poured down again, obscuring most of the details of the space. Gabe guided me over the remnants of a wall and down a flight of steps.

"Where are we?" I asked over the cascade of rain.

"This is where I live."

The rain began to lessen, slowing to a drizzle. I looked around. Barrels lined one of the walls, and a canvas awning extended from one of the others, providing a little shelter. Gabe headed for the awning, and I followed him.

Part of the wall beneath the awning had been hollowed out, making a cave-like space. It was filled with straw, with bedrolls and blankets shoved into the corners away from the rain. A fire burned in a metal pot on a stone ledge high above the straw, and a kettle dangled over it on a chain. A young man with thick black hair and a patch over one eye sat in the corner, reading a book. He looked up as we entered.

"This is Cathan," Gabe said, gesturing at him. "He's a member of the resistance, and a friend. Cat, this is Lia."

Cat's eyebrows lifted. "Lia...as in Weaver?"

"You've heard of me?" I said, surprised.

"Ah, yes," Cat said, his visible eye shifting to Gabe. His mouth curved up in a faint smirk. "He likes to talk about you."

"Cat!" Gabe's neck turned red, and he gave me a sheepish smile before glaring at his friend, who shrugged. He rose and went out, leaving us alone.

I was too tired and emotionally exhausted to ponder what that meant.

Gabe saw my expression and steered me toward one of the bedrolls. "Rest," he said, motioning for me to sit. "Let me have that coat. I'll hang it up to dry."

I peeled off the soaking fabric and handed it to him. My legs folded, and I sank down onto the straw. Gabe slung my coat and his over a rope stretched across the opening of the room. He retrieved a kettle from the fire and poured steaming liquid into a chipped mug. I accepted it gratefully when he returned.

"Now," Gabe said, sitting beside me on the straw. "Tell me. Why are you here? What's going on?"

He listened gravely as I recounted the incident with Gordon and the predicament I found myself in.

"Do you remember when Stone mentioned that man who'd spoken of me the night we were captured by the Wanderers?" I asked.

"I remember," he said, scowling. "I remember everything about that horrible night."

"I think that man he spoke about was Borde."

Gabe absorbed this information. He rubbed his hand across his face and looked away from me at the sky visible through the hole in the wall. "And why did you come to me?"

I took a deep breath. "I need help. I've already spoken to Adam, and he..." I stopped. A lump squeezed my throat, and I couldn't breathe for a moment. Pain shot through my veins, and I felt as though I were all alone after a hard fall.

"I've withdrawn from the Thorns," I whispered. "They cannot help me. I'm on my own."

Gabe was silent for a long moment. "Korr could find him, I'm sure of it. The Thorns may have cast you off, but the Restorationists have their own agenda, friends of the Thorns though we be. We might be able to do something."

The image of that sneering, dark-haired dandy flashed through my head. I recoiled. "No."

"Lia, he can help us." Gabe leaned forward, his expression earnest. "Just let me talk to him. He has contacts all over this city. If anyone can find out where someone's hiding, it's him."

"Absolutely not. He won't help me. He'll only use this against me."

Gabe lifted his head in excitement. "If you offer him your da's notebooks and journals—"

"They burned," I interrupted. "There was a fire. They are gone. I have nothing to bargain with."

"If we could just ask him—"

"No."

I held Gabe's gaze without comment until he looked away. I had plenty of reasons not to trust his brother, and he knew it as well as I did. I didn't know where all this unexpected loyalty had come from, but I didn't share it.

Gabe exhaled noisily and moved his hands restlessly against his knees. He brushed at a piece of hair hanging in his eyes and grimaced. "We'll do what we can without involving him. You know I'll do anything I can to help you."

"Thank you."

"Sleep," Gabe said. "We'll make more plans in the morning. We'll figure out exactly what needs to be done. I promise."

Exhaustion tugged at me. I lay down without another word and shut my eyes. I heard Cat return at some point, and he and Gabe conversed quietly. I fell asleep to the sound of their murmuring.

~

The world was bathed in white when I woke. The rain was gone, replaced by a faint mist that hung over everything and wrapped the buildings in gauzy tendrils. I sat up and looked around for Gabe, but he was gone. Cat stood by the fire pot, fiddling with the kettle.

"Tea?" he asked without turning around.

"Yes, please," I said, and shoved back the blankets Gabe must have put over me. Every muscle in my body ached. A headache pounded at the back of my skull. I rose with a groan.

"It's not the most comfortable bed in the world, but it gets the job done," Cat remarked. He handed me a steaming cup with a smile and a flick of his eyebrows.

"Where's Gabe?"

Cat sank down on the straw near me and blew on his tea to cool it. "He had something to attend to. I'm not sure what, but I'm on a need-to-know basis within the..." He stopped before finishing his sentence and jerked his shoulders in a shrug. "I'm supposed to be keeping you entertained until he gets back."

Did he think I didn't know about what Gabe was doing here?

"You're a Restorationist like Gabe, aren't you?"

Cat looked thoughtful. "Ah, so you know about the cause. But of course you do."

"How'd you lose the eye?" I asked, because I got the impression that he valued directness.

Cat grinned. "They thought they could torture answers out of me. They were wrong."

"They?"

"The Dictator's guards."

Footsteps clattered on the stones behind us, and Gabe appeared on the steps leading down into the courtyard. He carried a ragged bundle in his arms.

"Breakfast," he called out, tossing it to Cat.

Cat opened the bundle and held up a loaf of bread. My stomach knotted at the fresh scent wafting from it. He broke off a piece for me, and I tore into it.

"Good morning," Gabe said, sinking onto the straw beside me. "How did you sleep?"

"Not well," I said. I took another bite of the bread, chewing more slowly this time. It was coarse and filling. I swallowed the last bit and licked my fingers. I was still hungry.

"Me either," Gabe confessed, fiddling with his portion of the bread. He stole a glance at me as if looking for confirmation of something.

Across the room, Cat rolled his eyes and climbed to his feet. "That's my cue to leave, I suppose," he said, and strolled toward the door.

"Where's Claire?" I asked Gabe. "Didn't she come to Aeralis with you?"

Didn't she have claim to you? I wanted to add, but I didn't. The memory of his goodbye kiss burned on my lips—a kiss he'd given me in front of her.

Still, I didn't understand it. He cared for her, too. I wasn't the only person with mixed-up feelings.

Gabe hesitated until Cat left the shelter to perch at the edge of the courtyard wall. He leaned forward and lowered his voice.

"Clara is posing as a servant in Korr's house. I would be there as well, but as I told you before, Korr fears I'd be recognized because of my resemblance to him. Here, though..." He shrugged. "I can move freely most of the time. And when I can't, I grubby myself up with mud and soot and then nobody looks twice at me." Gabe hesitated, and his gaze shifted to Cat. "Korr's involvement as a Restorationist is a secret, even from other members of the organization. Only a few know of his true loyalties. Don't mention his name, ever. Not to anyone in the Thorns, not to any Restorationists, unless they already interact with him."

I nodded.

Cat returned for more tea, and Gabe conversed with him quietly about messages to be delivered and supplies to be acquired. I finished my tea and stood, stretching my sore muscles.

Gabe observed me from his place on the straw. "How long do you think you're going to stay?"

"Only until I can find Borde and this device of his," I said with a sigh. "Don't worry. I don't intend to overstay my welcome."

"You're always welcome," Gabe said.

Cat made a choking sound. When Gabe glared at him, he pounded his chest and coughed. "My tea went down the wrong pipe," he said, but his eyes were laughing.

Gabe muttered something that sounded suspiciously like an insult under his breath. Cat only grinned.

"How did you two meet?" I asked.

Gabe fiddled with the straw. "We knew each other as children. We were good friends, and still are."

"What he means to say," Cat said, "is that I was a servant in the palace, but he doesn't like to tell that part."

"Well, it makes you sound..." Gabe gestured at nothing with a scowl.

"Worthless?" Cat suggested.

"No. Never that. But I think it misrepresents what you were to me. A brother, really."

"Aw," Cat said, his flippant grin back now. "That's real touching."

I was amused by their interactions, but the distraction began to thin as the pressure of my mission weighed against me. "I need to find Borde, and quickly," I reminded Gabe. "We need a plan."

Gabe knit his fingers together and looked at the Aeralian skyline poking through the mist like leafless tree trunks. "I think we should start with some of our usual intelligence contacts. Ask around and see if anyone knows of a man by his name or description in the city."

I nodded.

His eyes softened as he looked at me again. "Have you eaten enough? It wasn't much, I know."

"We survived months of starvation together," I said. "The bread was more than fine."

He nodded. He reached for my hand, but his fingers stopped just above mine. I stared at them, not speaking. He sighed and turned away. "We should get going."

I followed him without a word.

~

I observed the swath of storm clouds above us warily as we left the tunnels and entered the Plaza of Horses. It was morning, but the plaza was still in shadows. "Is it always this way here?"

"It's not called the city of light for nothing," Gabe said, pointing at the flickering streetlights. "They burn day and night."

The streetlamps did little to dispel the gloom of the plaza. The carved horses rose from the fog like beasts ascending from a gray sea. The air was wet and too warm, and remnants of the rain dripped and splattered into puddles on the stones. Somewhere close, a bridle bit jingled, and a man shouted the time to his comrade.

"The plaza was built to commemorate the end of the Aerialian civil war a hundred years ago." Gabe hesitated and dropped his voice. "The Prison District was not always so large," he said. "This used to be a happy place. People would bring picnic lunches here. They often held concerts or had poetry readings in the evenings. I loved this place. Now look at it."

"I'm sorry," I said, words supremely inadequate for the vastness of his sorrow. However, I understood what it was like to have a beloved place hollowed out by an occupation. That solidarity wrapped us in warm silence as we crossed the plaza.

We reached the wall, and Gabe motioned to where a stone arch opened onto a street. "This way."

We slipped through the streets, moving from one streetlamp to the next as a faint mist drifted down from the sky and made my coat and hair damp. Moisture gathered in Gabe's hair and beaded on his lashes. He looked at me often, but he didn't say anything else.

We entered a part of the city crowded with pedestrians and carriages. Children darted in the streets, and sellers hawked wares from shops crowded under low-hanging roofs that shielded them from rain. Gabe grabbed my hand and tugged me forward into the chaos. My fingers tingled against his, and I considered pulling away, but I didn't want to lose him in the crowd. I let him lead me until we'd reached the corner of the street, and then he looked at me and dropped my hand.

"Sorry," he muttered. "Habit."

"Where are we?"

"I have a contact here," he said. "He can find out anything I need to know. I'll ask him to find Borde, and he'll do it. He can find anything."

"Are you sure?"

"I'm sure," Gabe said.

We entered an alley. At the back, next to where rainwater poured through a spout into a barrel, was a crooked blue door. As we approached it, the knob rattled, and then it creaked open. Half of a face peered out. I caught a glimpse of a tangle of long, dark hair, a flash of teeth as crooked as the door, and a thin and shrewd face. The young man couldn't have been any older than Adam, I decided, and pain shot through me like a knife at the thought of him.

"Gabe," the young man said. "And someone I don't know." He said it like it was an accomplishment that he'd identified me as such.

"Ferris," Gabe greeted him. "This is Lia."

"A pleasure," Ferris said, turning in my direction.

That was when I realized he was blind.

ELEVEN

"HOW CAN HE work if he's blind?" I asked Gabe as we left the alley. We entered the stream of people in the street, and I grabbed Gabe's arm to keep from being separated. Gabe looked at my hand out of the corner of his eye, and his arm tensed, but he didn't comment on our contact.

"Ferris hears things others do not," he said. "The soldiers ignore him because of his blindness, and because of that, he has freedom to move and listen. He is clever and quick, and his ears are sharp. You'll forget that he cannot see after a while, once you get to know him. It doesn't matter, really. He doesn't let it matter."

The subject matter made me think of Jonn, and my chest clenched. He had been willing to risk death to change his condition, and the Sickness had not healed him as he'd hoped. And Ivy...

I could not think of it now. It took all my strength to focus on the scene before me.

We rounded the corner and reached a plaza that reminded me of the Plaza of Horses, except this one was smaller and the statues were all of men.

"The Plaza of Poets," Gabe explained when he saw me looking around. "These are all famous Aeralian writers. Gerraris, Simalade..."

I didn't know any of the poets he was listing, but that hardly mattered. What use did I have for poets?

A dry fountain sat in the middle of the plaza. Leaves and debris filled the place that had once held water. I stopped beside it and looked down. A few inches of brackish rainwater puddled in the lowest places. My reflection stared back at me. I looked Aeralian, with my long dark coat with the brass buttons and my knotted hair.

"Come on," Gabe said. "I know a few more places where we can inquire."

I followed him down the street. A cloud of steam enveloped us, and as we crossed the street, I thought I saw the flutter of a coat disappearing around a corner. My heartbeat spiked, but when I looked again, there was no one there.

We searched up and down the streets, looking for the white-haired scientist, asking for a man called Meridus Borde. People shook their heads at our description and made blank faces at his name.

"Meridus?" One shopkeeper scratched his chin and stared off at the rainy sky above us. "I seem to recall a fellow by that name. Older man. Last name was Falcon. But I don't know where he went. He didn't stay in this area long."

"Thanks," I mumbled. Who knew how many Meriduses might live in this city?

After hours of fruitless searching, we rested our weary feet in a crowded tavern at the edge of the prison sector, near the Plaza of Horses and Gabe's makeshift home. Rowdy patrons pushed around us, yelling for songs from the performing minstrel and spilling drinks.

"Don't worry," Gabe said, watching my expression as he took a sip of his drink. "Ferris will find something. I'm sure of it."

I stared at the mug before me. There was still time, but it was rapidly slipping away. Anxiety tightened its cold fingers around my heart and squeezed. I took a couple of deep breaths and tried to look calm.

"Lia." Gabe covered my hand with his. "We'll find him."

I nodded. I thought of Adam and our stormy parting, and part of me burned with rage. Another part of me curled up in misery and wanted comfort.

Irritated at my conflicted feelings, I gulped my drink. The liquid burned going down. I pushed the mug away and dropped my head in my hands. "There just isn't much time."

"I'll ask some of the people here," Gabe said, and rose from his place.

He crossed the room, tapping on shoulders and whispering in ears. Most of the diners shrugged their shoulders or shook their heads. A few were more belligerent.

"Get off," one man yelled, swinging his fist at Gabe. "I came here for a little relaxation. Don't bother me."

Gabe retreated to our table. He gave me a shaky smile. "Some of these people are less than friendly at the end of the day," he said.

"So I see."

Someone dropped into the chair opposite us. A man with dark eyes and darker hair. His skin was chiseled with wrinkles, and they folded around his eyes as he squinted at Gabe.

"You've been asking a lot of questions," he said.

"We're looking for someone."

"I see. Well, around here, we don't like people asking too many questions. It stirs up trouble, and trouble brings soldiers. We don't like the soldiers. See?"

"We understand," I said. "We were just going actually." I stood, and Gabe followed suit.

"Wait," the man said, leaning forward. "You look familiar." He clapped a hand on Gabe's shoulder and pushed him back into his seat. "Why do you look so familiar?"

I froze. Gabe didn't say anything. We stared at the man, and he stared at us.

"I just can't place it," he muttered.

"A lot of people say that," Gabe said. He looked at me.

I jerked my head toward the door, and he nodded. He bolted from his chair, and we both ran.

"Hey!" the man shouted. He jumped up and started after us, snagging Gabe's sleeve, and Gabe turned and punched him. The man went down in a clatter of chairs and a string of curses.

We reached the outside and went left, running into the mist. We didn't stop until we'd put three blocks between the tavern and us.

"Do you think he recognized you?" I asked when I had my breath back.

Gabe shook his head. "No. He'll forget it tomorrow."

"And if he doesn't?"

Gabe didn't answer that. "Let's go home. It's late. We'll meet Ferris in the morning and see what he's dug up on your friend Borde."

~

The next morning, we slipped through the misty streets to Ferris's door. I knocked with shaking fingers and waited, my stomach a riot of nerves, until the sound of footsteps echoed on the other side of the door. The knob turned, and Ferris poked his head out and tipped it to one side, listening to us breathe and inhaling the air around us.

"Gabe," he said after a pause. "And your friend again?"

"The same," Gabe said. "Do you have any information for us?"

Ferris leaned against the doorframe and tapped his finger against the button on his sleeve. "I found a name," he said. "Meridus Falcon, he's calling himself now."

"We heard that name yesterday," I said. "It isn't the right man."

"Oh," Ferris said. "But it is. According to my contacts, an older man with a scarred face came with a companion into the city recently. He originally gave his name as Borde, then seemed to reconsider that and told a few people to contact him by the name of Falcon. You have your man, I think. He's using an alias."

"Falcon," I repeated. "So he's here."

"He's here," Ferris assured me.

"But you don't know where?"

"After that, he completely vanished. Might have gone into one of the nicer districts. I don't have contacts there."

Gabe paid him, and we left. My mind reeled as I absorbed this new information. Borde was using another name—Falcon. And not even Ferris knew where he was now.

"Who else can we talk to? Who else might know Borde's whereabouts?"

Gabe shook his head.

Despair filled me like water flooding my lungs. Jonn was going to die, Ivy was going to die, and I was going to be here when it happened, trapped in a city of fog and light, unable to find the man I needed to save them. In my mind's eye, I saw them, both sick, him lying under a quilt, his bones thin and brittle as sticks beneath his skin, his eyes open and bloodshot, his mouth a gash in his gaunt face as he gasped for his last lungful of air. Her sunk down on her knees beside him, sick but not as sick, not yet, holding out till the last for Jonn's sake. Waiting for me. Hoping in vain.

Every inch of me hurt. My legs weakened, and I crumpled into a crouch beside the fountain and braced myself against the stones, trying to breathe.

Gabe dropped down beside me and reached for my hand. I let him take my fingers. His skin was warm against mine.

"I know another man," he said after a long silence. "It's a gamble, but he might know something. But..." He paused. "It's a risk. He lives near the palace, in one of the wealthier neighborhoods. If I'm recognized..."

Our eyes met. I felt my soul pouring out of mine, pleading with him even as I wrestled with the risk.

Gabe sighed, the sound scraping past his lips.

"Come on," he said.

~

Brittle vines trailed down the sides of the buildings in this part of the city, and ancient trees snaked their roots over walls of stone and transparent roofs with vegetation inside—greenhouses like the one back in the Frost. Steam powered the coaches, and the men and women who strolled by on foot wore black silk and velvet. Feathered and veiled hats hid their eyes.

One man passing us made eye contact. The haunted fear in his face rocked me, and I stopped in the middle of the street. Gabe grabbed my arm and pulled me forward onto the sidewalk, hustling me away quickly before the man could look again. I shook off the spell that had gripped me as we slipped through a gate and stopped before a house with curving stone walls topped with pointed iron spikes.

Gabe's expression was a mixture of wonder and unease, as if he'd stepped into an unsettling dream. "I haven't seen these walls since before my arrest," he murmured.

He led me down a path and through a grove of drooping trees. We passed through a hedge and into a courtyard of raked gravel. Dried leaves skittered past us, swirling in a sudden wind. We skirted the house and headed deeper into the surrounding gardens. Dried vines drooped from the trees and brushed the top of my head. The air smelled like wet dirt and dead plants. Thunder growled in the distance, a whisper of another coming storm.

"Here." Gabe pointed toward a flight of stairs leading along the back of the house, descending into a concealed area beneath the garden. I followed him down the steps and into a place that resembled a cave. Coils of wire and glass vials lined the walls. A great broken clock lay on its side on a table.

"Gabriel?"

A shadow stirred in the corner by a table, and a man with white hair moved into the light, squinting at us.

"Gabriel," he repeated. "Is that you?"

"Dr. Terrade," Gabe said, and his voice came out quick and breathless. "I don't have time to explain."

"We thought you were dead," the white-haired man said. His eyes shifted to my face. He wore an expression of curiousness and suspicion.

"It's a long story," Gabe said. "But I need your help, and there's no time to explain. Have you ever met or heard of a man who calls himself Meridus Falcon?"

My chest tightened as the old man tipped his head to the side and thought about it.

"Meridus Falcon," he mused. "For some reason, that seems familiar, but I can't recall anything specific."

"It's important," I said firmly. "Think harder."

Terrade swiveled his neck to get a better look at me. His eyes blinked, turtle-like. "And who are you?"

"Lila," Gabe answered for me, using the name I'd taken after I'd traveled through the gate to the old time before the Frost. "She's a friend of mine."

"Lila," Terrade repeated. He gave me a searching look as if he were tasting the name on his tongue and finding it unfamiliar to his palate. He pulled a scrap of paper from his pocket and scribbled something on it. "Any friend of Gabriel's is a friend of mine." His own words distracted him, and he gazed into space, murmuring them under his breath. He blinked. "Excuse me. What were we discussing?"

"Meridus Falcon," Gabe reminded him.

"Ah, yes." Terrade ambled across the room to a row of cluttered shelves. Muttering to himself again, he began to pull books and bits of paper from them and lay the pieces in neat rows across a worktable. One of the papers fluttered to the ground and lay there, forgotten amid his flurry of activity.

"What's he doing?" I asked.

"He writes everything down," Gabe said. "Records and observations, names, dates. He pours through the papers, he keeps his own journals—he's obsessive. He keeps his finger on the pulse of the city. It's a hobby, a quirk. I don't know why he does it, but he's been doing it all my life."

"You knew him before?"

Gabe nodded. His lips tightened in a way that suggested he didn't want to talk about it, not now.

I wondered who this man had been to him, what they'd shared.

"Ah," Terrade said, holding up a scrap of paper in triumph. "Meridus Falcon."

"What does it say?" I demanded. My heart began to pound with nervous anticipation. Sweat broke across my palms.

Terrade squinted at the writing. "He was...oh dear."

"What? What is it?"

The doctor lifted his head. "According to this record, a Meridus Falcon was arrested and imprisoned on charges of treason several weeks ago." He held out a piece of paper to Gabe.

Arrested. Treason. My stomach twisted into a hard ball of horror. I opened my mouth to speak.

That was when the soldiers kicked down the door.

TWELVE

GABE THREW HIMSELF toward Dr. Terrade's table of parchments and papers as the soldiers entered the room, weapons drawn. Terrade let out a shriek as one of the soldiers struck him. He crumpled into a heap on the floor, and they hauled him up. Another seized Gabe and yanked him around, and I saw he'd somehow managed to splatter ink all over his face and shirt, concealing his identity. The soldier made a sound of disgust as ink got all over his hands and the front of his uniform.

Rough hands twisted my arms behind my back and forced me toward the door.

"Lia!" Gabe shouted.

I couldn't do anything. I bit my lip to keep from screaming as they forced me outside. I couldn't think. Couldn't breathe.

We were captured.

It would all be over soon.

The soldiers marched us forward across the garden, toward the front of the house. There were three of them, all grim-faced and gray-clad. Their guns glittered in the pale light.

Something fluttered out of the corner of my eye. I turned my head in time to see a man in a black coat smash one of the soldiers in the face with a tree limb. Gabe kneed one of the other soldiers, and the man crumpled at the unexpected attack. I drove my elbow into the throat of the soldier behind me.

"Go!" shouted the man in the black coat, and I realized it was Adam.

I struggled. One of the soldiers smashed the butt of his gun into my face, and everything went black.

~

Pain laced every breath I took. My head throbbed. I licked my lips and tasted blood.

"Lia? Are you all right?"

Gabe's frantic whisper came somewhere from my left. My hands slid over smooth leather as I pushed myself upright. "Well. I'm alive."

The ground lurched beneath us. We were in a carriage. I opened my eyes, squinting against the light. Everything was too bright, too blurry. "How long was I unconscious?"

"Not long," Gabe said. "A few minutes. Are you all right?"

"Yes, that nasty cut above your eye looks painful," another voice interjected. "It's rather marred what looks you had. Pity. And you're going to have a terrific bruise tomorrow."

Korr.

I touched the side of my face with two fingers, probing the injured flesh gently as I squinted at the other occupants of the carriage. I could just make out the nobleman. "Where are we?" I demanded.

"My steamcoach," he said in a clipped tone.

My vision finally adjusted, and I could see them all.

Korr crossed his legs and scowled at the velvet ceiling of the steamcoach. Gabe slumped between his brother and Dr. Terrade's still form. His face was still splotched with ink. And beside me...

Adam.

"You," I said.

Adam turned his body away from me and set his face toward the window. His fingers moved restlessly over the edge of his cloak, and he scanned my face again. He didn't speak.

"How did you find us?" Gabe asked finally.

Korr pursed his lips as if choosing just the right words. "Luckily, Brewer has been following Weaver. Who knows what could have happened otherwise?"

"Following me?" I demanded.

A muscle in Adam's jaw flexed. "You said you wanted out of the Thorns, and as a Thorns agent I couldn't stop you from making that choice. But I wasn't about to let you wander around Astralux alone without someone keeping an eye on you. What kind of man do you think I am?"

"How dare you follow me without my permission?" I snapped. "How did you even—?" I glared at Gabe. "Did you know about this?"

He said nothing, but his forehead wrinkled and his eyes shifted guiltily.

"How do you think he found you?" Adam asked, still not looking at me.

"So you told Gabe where I was? That's how he found me at the Plaza of Horses?"

"Never mind that." Korr leaned forward as the steamcoach rattled over a pothole. "The point is that you've both been exceptionally stupid. Without our intervention, Gabriel would have been identified, and nobody can know he's alive. Not to mention the fact that you both would have been executed, perhaps tortured beforehand, and I'm sure I don't need to convince you of the unpleasantness of that."

I didn't care about Korr's temper tantrum. I was looking at Adam.

Instead of returning my stare, he squinted at the street through the dark glass of the steamcoach, his forehead knit with an unidentifiable emotion. I reached for his hand to get his attention, and he flinched. I drew mine away quickly.

The steamcoach stopped with a lurch and a hiss. Through the tinted glass of the coach windows, the moon glimmered amid the night mist that blanketed the streets. Streetlamps glowed like small fires in the distance. Korr leaned across Gabe and slid the window open to speak to the driver.

"Drive around back," he ordered, and sat back with a longsuffering sigh. He looked at us all as if he were dealing with idiots. "We can't be seen," he said. "Especially not you two." He waved his fingers at Gabe and me. "Cover your faces with your coats."

The steamcoach stopped before a back entrance. Korr lifted the still-unconscious Dr. Terrade and climbed from the coach. I followed Korr, holding the lapels of my coat up to cover my profile. Structures of glass glittered to our left, and flowering trees drooped over a doorway. Gabe and Adam were behind me, and I heard Adam mutter something to Gabe under his breath. It didn't sound friendly, but I didn't catch what was said.

We entered a supply room. Shelves covered the walls. High windows let in strips of moonlight. Korr disappeared into another room, and I heard him barking orders at servants to fetch water. He returned without Terrade and lit a gas lamp beside the door with a flick of his finger. He paused for a moment, staring at the flame as if deciding who to shout at first, and then he turned on us. He pointed a gloved hand at Gabe and me.

"What shall we talk about first? Your utter stupidity, or how furious I am?"

"Korr—" Gabe started.

"Shut up. I want to hear what Weaver has to say."

My heart stuttered at the cold fire burning in his eyes. I swallowed and didn't speak.

"We're going to talk about how to proceed from here," Adam interjected calmly. He shut the door behind him and leaned against it. Korr gave him a wrathful glance but didn't argue. He crossed his arms and looked at us both expectantly.

Gabe sank onto a barrel. "It's my fault. Don't yell at her."

"No, it's my fault," I said.

"It was my idea to go to Terrade. I thought he could help us."

"I want to know what's going on," Korr said. "Why is Weaver in Astralux? What were you doing talking to Dr. Terrade? Start at the beginning."

"My family business is none of yours," I snapped.

"So it's a Weaver affair," he said, his eyes narrowing with contemplation.

I clamped my lips shut. How had I let that slip?

"You're poking around my city and attracting attention with your escapades, and that makes it my affair," he said. "So start talking."

I shook my head. I wouldn't trust Korr with my least-favorite pair of snowshoes, and he wanted me to put my siblings' lives in his hands? "I have absolutely no reason to offer that information to you."

"I just saved your life," he growled. "You owe me."

"He did help us, Lia," Gabe ventured.

I gave Gabe a look that silenced him and turned back to Korr.

"I owe you nothing," I managed through clenched teeth. "You never do anything out of the goodness of your heart, so you must have some kind of ulterior motive for rescuing me."

"I rescued my brother, too," he pointed out. "Perhaps you are just exceptionally lucky to have been captured with him."

"I don't think so," I said. "You always arrange it so there's a benefit to you."

His furious face softened into one of faint amusement. "Well," he drawled, "I suppose I do." His gaze cut to Gabe and then back to me. "I rather like you, Weaver, when I'm not hating you."

Now there was a compliment I'd never wanted to receive. I scowled at him. "Well, I don't like you, and I'm not telling you anything. I know you want something from me."

A smile crawled across his face, but it didn't reach his eyes. They were dark and hard with determination. "Your father's journals."

"No," I said. "I told you before."

His eyes hardened. "That isn't your final answer."

"You're wrong."

"Do I need to remind you that I saved your life? That I am harboring you here in my house out of the goodness of my heart?"

"What goodness?" I countered.

Korr's gloved fingers flexed. "Fine. I'll throw you out if you don't give them to me."

Adam shifted. "Korr," he said, and there was an undercurrent of something sharp lurking in his tone.

"She can't," Gabe said. "They burned."

Korr looked at his brother. His face transformed into something terrifying. He turned back to me.

"Is this true?"

I swallowed hard. "Yes. They're gone."

Korr swore. He looked at me. "Right now you need to disappear from my sight while I figure out how to fix this."

He locked eyes with Adam, and something unspoken passed between them, some communication.

Even Korr had more rapport with Adam right now than I did.

"Upstairs," Korr snapped, turning his attention back to me as if I were some errant child.

I was too exhausted to argue further.

~

Korr showed me to a guest room to sleep. I was surprised at first that he didn't ask a servant to do it, but then I remembered I wasn't supposed to be here.

The guest room had striped wallpaper and a velvet canopy bed. The scent of roses hung in the air, and I caught a glimpse of myself in the mirror over the bureau. My face was wild and dirty, my hair a snarl. I looked half-dead with fatigue.

"Is there a story yet to explain my presence if anyone sees me?" I asked, turning to where Korr lounged in the doorway.

"My mistress," he said with a rude smile.

"Absolutely not."

"Believe me when I say I'm joking," he said. "You can pose as a servant for now."

I spread my hands to indicate the lavish decorations. "Would a servant stay in a room like this?"

"Not any servant," he said, arching his eyebrow with an angry smile. "My personal assistant. That way you'll be close enough to keep an eye on at all times."

He shut the door with a slam before I could say anything else, leaving me to deal with that unpleasant declaration in addition to everything else that had gone wrong that day. I went to the bed and sank onto it. I tugged off my boots and shrugged out of my dirty coat. My muscles throbbed. My mind reeled. I fell back against the mattress and put my hands over my eyes.

I needed to bathe and sleep before I tried to come up with any plans about what I'd do to get out of this situation.

A quiet knock came at the door, and I raised my head with a growl of annoyance. I had no more patience for Korr's games tonight.

The knob turned, and Gabe stepped inside. He shut the door and leaned against it.

"I'm sorry," he said. "I shouldn't have taken you to Terrade. I was stupid."

"Don't. It's happened; it's done." I sat up and rubbed the space between my eyes. Worry was already gnawing at my gut like a rat. Right before the soldiers had burst through the door, Terrade had said Borde had been arrested. Any hope I'd been harboring was rapidly dwindling to nothing.

Gabe shook his head at my words. "No. I acted foolishly. I should have known better than to return to that part of the city. Of course they were watching his house. He was a friend of my family, and the Dictator is notoriously suspicious of his nobles. And if I'd been recognized, we would have probably been shot on sight." He stared at the floor. "I'm sorry about your being forced to stay here with my brother. I know you despise him."

"Never mind Korr," I said. "What are we going to do about Borde?"

A wrinkle of comprehension crossed Gabe's face. "Dr. Terrade gave me that paper just before we were arrested. If I still have it..." He thrust his hands into the pockets of his vest and pants, searching. He fished out a wadded scrap of white and held it to the light. "Yes, this is it."

"What does it say?" I demanded.

"It says, 'Meridus Falcon, arrested on charges of treason on the anniversary of His Eminence's rise to power and sentenced to a life's internment in one of the work camps.'" He closed his fingers into a fist around the paper.

"Work camps?" I asked, my heart in my throat.

"The people call them death camps. They're mostly located outside the city. The Dictator sends prisoners there to, well, die."

Despair flooded me. I sucked in a breath and tried to make a plan, but my thoughts stuck together.

Gabe shifted his feet. "If I asked Korr—"

"No," I snapped. "I don't want him involved. He can't help us. He'll only try to use this to manipulate me further."

Gabe looked like he wanted to argue, so I told him I was tired. After he left, I shut my eyes and dropped back onto the bed. I was filthy; I needed to wash. But at the moment, I didn't care. I pushed back the coverlet and crawled beneath it. As I shut my eyes, I heard a knock at the door.

Gabe again?

This time, it was Adam who stepped inside. His dark eyes held mine, and fire burned inside me. Part of me was aching to run to him, but another part of me was furious. I did not rise from the bed. I stared at him, he stared at me, and neither of us spoke. A desire for comfort did battle with my anger, and my anger won.

"So," I finally said, and the word was a challenge.

"I know you are angry—"

"How dare you tail me like I'm some suspect your organization wants to spy upon? Who ordered you to do it?"

"I didn't do it as a Thorns operative," he said. "I did it as someone who was worried about your safety."

"Don't make decisions for me, Brewer."

He winced.

I ran a hand over the coverlet. "You should go. I doubt it's proper for you to be here."

"Actually," he said. "I only came to bring someone else."

Ann stepped around the door, and I inhaled sharply as a burning filled my eyes. I shoved back the covers and stumbled toward her. She met me halfway and fell into my arms, and I clutched at her hair and the sleeves of her clothing to assure myself she was real. She put her head on my shoulder and squeezed me tight. When I looked over her head at the door, Adam was gone.

"He told me what happened," Ann said when she'd released me. "What are you going to do?"

I went to the bed and sank onto it. My legs were too tired to support me any longer. "I don't know," I admitted, and saying the words punctured a hole in the last bit of bravado I had left.

"Lia," she said gently.

"I came to find Borde," I said. "Did Adam tell you that?"

"Yes."

"Gabe and I went to a man who knew something. He said a man named Meridus Falcon had been arrested for treason weeks ago. He's in a work camp. A *death* camp, Ann. What am I going to do? Jonn and Ivy are going to die."

"We'll figure something out," she whispered, and hugged me tighter.

THIRTEEN

WHEN I OPENED my eyes the next morning, I found a girl in a gray servant's uniform standing beside the bed, watching me with a fixed expression of total disinterest and holding a stack of fabric in her arms. There was something familiar about her, but my sleep-fogged mind couldn't make the connection.

"Good morning," she said when I sat up. "Here are your linens and extra uniforms. Lord Korr had them sent up. He said you'd need them right away."

I groaned at the memory that he'd made me his personal assistant. "Put them on the bed, please."

She set the clothes and other things down at the foot of the bed and crossed the room to open the curtains. "Servants usually rise at six," she said, and a smirk tinged her tone.

Raven.

I pushed back the blankets and slid out of bed. The carpet was warm beneath my bare feet.

"What are you doing here?" I asked.

"I'm posing as a servant in service to the Thorns. Or maybe I just think the uniforms here are rather fetching on me. What do you think?" She turned and put her hands on her hips.

"You're working with Adam?"

She smirked and didn't reply. She went to the door and shut it behind her, leaving me alone with the unsettling feeling of jealousy.

I put on one of the uniforms she'd brought. There was a pair of black, wide-legged trousers and a white linen blouse with ruffles at the throat, the only thing that marked it as feminine. A vest studded with brass buttons went over the blouse. I was buttoning it when a knock came at the door. My eyes widened slightly as a thin, red-haired young woman slipped inside. She paused at the sight of me. "They didn't tell me it was *you*."

"Claire." Her name came out through gritted teeth. She was not as thin as she'd been the last time we'd seen each other, but her eyes still had a skittish, hungry look in them.

She kept her expression blank. "I go by Clara here."

I shouldn't have been surprised by her appearance. It was only sensible for her to be here. She'd left the Frost with Gabe months ago, and they were close friends. Of course she'd joined the Restorationists.

Still, I hadn't expected her to walk through my door.

"Lord Korr said his new assistant was staying here."

"That's what they're calling me," I said stiffly.

"I came to inform you that breakfast will be served in the glass hall today."

"I'm not hungry."

"Suit yourself," she said, and left the room.

~

The rain hadn't abated, so I couldn't go outside to think. I ached for the windswept skies and stark beauty of the Frost. Something about the clean white blankness of snow always cleared my mind. Instead, I wandered until I found a door that led to a glass room filled with plants. A greenhouse? Rain splattered on the transparent roof and dripped down the walls. I pushed through the flowering branches that hung over the path and found a bench. I sank onto the cool stone and dropped my head in my hands.

I froze as I heard voices. Footsteps crunched on a path behind me. I turned, but I couldn't see who was coming through the trees.

"I'm impatient to hear we're still waiting around, making small talk with duchesses at parties instead of leading the revolution."

I didn't recognize the voice.

"Soon," another voice purred, one that I did know. Korr. I strained to hear. "Tell them to be patient. There are matters of delicacy that must be resolved."

"Matters." The first voice sounded less than thrilled to be given the brush-off. "What matters?"

"The instruments of our liberation are complicated," Korr said. "Patience."

The other man made a noise of annoyance, but he didn't press the matter.

My mind spun with thoughts long after they'd left the greenhouse. *Matters of delicacy that must be resolved. The instruments of our liberation are complicated.*

An idea sparked in my mind.

~

"Korr!"

He and Adam were bent over his desk, speaking in low tones as they examined a map. They both straightened as I stopped in the middle of his plush rug and crossed my arms.

"Yes?" He said it crisply, impatiently. He appeared to be in the middle of something and even shorter on patience than usual. Maybe I could use that.

I didn't waste any time stating what I had put together.

"You have the PLD, but you haven't used it," I said. "Because you need to use the gate at Echlos, too. I'm guessing you wanted my father's journals so you could learn how to link them. Now, why would you want to do that?"

Korr folded his arms and said nothing.

"To transport soldiers?" I continued. "The PLD is small and can be easily deployed inside a building." I paused. "Or a palace."

Korr said nothing as he gazed at me, his eyes black with an undefinable emotion.

"But you have to have it properly linked to the gate, so that passage through the gate will link travelers with the gate created by the PLD," I continued. "And right now the gate only takes people back in time. It's a matter of delicacy that must be resolved, yes?" I said, using the same words Korr had used in the greenhouse.

Korr stiffened as he realized I'd overheard him, that he wouldn't be able to lie to me. Still, he said nothing.

I had to focus. I had to be clear when presenting my idea, the idea I'd had after overhearing Korr earlier. "You need something that can show you how to reprogram the gate," I said. "You thought you could use my father's journals. The journals are gone. They burned. However, I can do you one better. I know of a *man* who could do it."

The room was silent for the space of several heartbeats while I waited for his response. Korr stirred slightly and lifted one gloved hand to his chin. His eyebrows drew together in a slash above his nose as he pinned me with a stare.

"A man?"

"Yes. He's—he's here in Astralux, but he's in trouble."

Korr smiled shrewdly as he observed my expression. I was struggling to keep it blank, but something of the desperation I felt must have leaked through my eyes, my posture, because he said, "This man, he has some personal significance to you. This is why you're in Astralux in the first place, isn't it? Who is he?"

"That doesn't concern this deal I'm offering you. The point is that he's being held in a labor camp, and I need him freed, but I can't do it alone. If you help me, I'll help you. I'll convince him to fix the gate. He'll listen to me."

It was a gamble; I wasn't entirely sure that Borde would help Korr, and I wasn't sure Korr would believe me anyway. But I had to try.

Korr's eyes narrowed. I was a prisoner to his stare, a bird to his snake. The seconds ticked past, marked by a clock on the wall, and my heart beat in time with them. Korr stepped around the desk and paced to a window that overlooked the street. He moved the curtain aside and gazed at the palace in the distance, then exchanged a long glance with Adam while I held my breath and pretended I wasn't coming apart at the seams, like an old barn battered by icy wind. My blood hummed. My back prickled with sweat.

Korr turned back to his desk. "All right."

Two words, spoken sharp and low—they might be the thing that saved my family. I put out a hand to brace myself against the wall as my legs sagged in relief.

"All right," I said, struggling to keep my voice calm. "What now?"

"Well, where is he?"

"Working on it," I said.

"Get me the name of the camp where he's being held, and we'll make our plans," Korr said. He waved a hand, and I was dismissed.

I left the room, still shaking.

A footstep made me turn. Adam had followed me out into the hall.

"Good thinking," he said, his voice unreadable. "Brilliant, really."

I didn't reply. Part of me wanted to ask him for advice, tell him my plans, or share my musings, but there was a rift between us. Our old camaraderie had been replaced with something new, something painful. It was as if a part of me had been amputated. I bled regret for the loss of him as we stood there, but I was silent. He was silent, too.

Adam turned to go back into the room. He paused at the door. "Talk to Raven if you need information. She has connections everywhere. She'll find out where he is. Ask her to do it as a favor to me. She owes me one."

Were they so close that they owed each other favors now? Something uncomfortable prickled in my chest.

Adam turned and went back into the study before I could ask anything, and I wouldn't have known what to ask anyway. Words lay thick on my tongue, but I swallowed them and went to find the information I needed.

FOURTEEN

DOCTOR TERRADE WAS still rattled from his ordeal the night before. He sipped tea on the couch of his guest suite as I tried to ask him questions about the man called Meridus Falcon. His hands shook as he lifted the teacup to his lips.

"I've told you all I know," he said repeatedly. "He's been arrested for treason. It was on the paper."

"Yes," I said, shutting my eyes to gather my patience. "But can you tell me anything else? Something you didn't write down, perhaps? What else do you remember?"

His bitter laugh turned into a wheeze. "I can't remember any of it. That's why I write it all down. My memory is failing me, so I keep record of every conversation, every snippet of gossip I hear at parties and social functions these days, and I read them over when I return home. It's become useful to some other people for reasons I'd rather not know, but I cannot help you further. I only have my notes, and that is all I have written regarding this Meridus Falcon."

I went to find Raven.

~

Raven studied me as I explained what I needed her to find out. She smiled at the mention of Adam and favors, but she didn't comment further on that.

"Falcon, eh?" she said when I'd finished. "He and I should meet. We'd be two birds of a feather." She grinned at her joke, but I didn't.

Her smile rearranged itself into her customary smirk at my lack of expression.

"Can you do it?" I asked. I had no patience for her today.

She shrugged. "There are men who have that information, and men are always eager to tell me things. I have a Thorns mission tonight—a gala at the home of the Head of Records. I'll find out your information."

"I'm coming with you."

She dimpled. "You? What would you do at an Aeralian party? There are no monsters to slay, Bluewing. Only men."

I wouldn't let her mocking dissuade me. "This is important," I said. "I want to make sure you do it right."

She laughed. "I know how to do my job, Frostie. I don't need you looking over my shoulder."

I simply folded my arms.

"All right," she said, giving me a measuring look. "I leave for the party at sunset. Be ready if you plan to come along."

I nodded, and she slipped past me and down the hall without another word.

"Lia."

I turned; Gabe stepped from the library.

"I guess I'm going to my first Aeralian party," I said.

Gabe dropped his gaze to his hands. "I heard. At the home of the Head of Records, no less. Edmund Steelgray. He has a fine conservatory. One of the finest in Aeralis." He hesitated. "I need you to do something for me."

My instincts sharpened as foreboding pierced me. I waited for him to explain.

"There's something at the Steelgray estate that I need. But I can't go. I'd be recognized. And I can't ask Raven—I don't trust her, and no one else can know about this."

"Not even Korr?"

"Not him," Gabe said. "Especially not him. Please, Lia."

"What is this thing you need so desperately?"

"It's a book of records."

I waited for him to tell me more, but he didn't. He chewed his lip and waited for me to refuse. I could see by his expression he thought I would. Mistrust stirred in my stomach—I'd had a lifetime's worth of betrayal in the last year—but along with it came memories of Gabe at my side in the Frost, climbing through windows, risking his life to help my family, my village.

I sighed. I owed him this, at least.

"Tell me where I can find it."

"Truly?"

"Yes, truly."

He stepped closer to me, and we were inches apart. I put out my hands. I could feel the heat of his skin even though we weren't touching. His eyes became soft, and the naked vulnerability that colored his features made me ache. I'd caused this sadness. I'd caused his tentative hope, and his heartbreak.

A shiver of regret and self-loathing curled inside me, but I pushed it away. I wouldn't dwell on that now. I reached out and touched his hand with mine. His skin was warm. Sparks slipped up my arm, and I shut my eyes.

"We are still friends, Gabe."

"Friends." He pronounced it bitterly. But when I tried to withdraw my hand, he captured my fingers with his and pulled me forward until my hand was resting against his chest. I opened my eyes in surprise.

"Lia," he breathed.

It was too much. Inside I was splintering with pain and drowning with the warm ache of want. But he wasn't—I wasn't—

Adam.

Even though we were barely speaking, his name still filled my mind.

I drew away from Gabe. "We shouldn't talk about this now. There's no time, and I..." I didn't have the slightest idea what to say to him.

"You're right," Gabe said, sighing quietly as he stepped back. "Let me tell you how to find the study were the records are kept."

~

Darkness blanketed the city, punctured at intervals by glowing glass streetlamps that lined the river. Fog hung heavy in the air above us.

The dress I wore dug painfully into my sides and itched at my shoulder blades where a cascade of lace fell down my back like a pair of tattered angel wings. My hair was heaped atop my head and strung with pearls—paste knock-offs, Raven had informed me, although they looked real—and I wore a mask of gray satin.

"You look like a regular Aeralian," Raven had announced upon seeing me, which was the best compliment she seemed capable of bestowing.

Gabe had been more admiring. He'd met me in the hall for last-minute instructions about my side mission on his behalf, and the sight of me in Ann's dress had rendered him speechless. He'd finally managed to drag his eyes away and review with me what I needed to do.

I, however, felt like a child playing pretend in her mother's gown. Even though the dress fit my body well, I didn't know the person I'd seen in the mirror. I'd worn cloaks stained and torn from passage through the Frost for so long that I didn't recognize myself without them. But Gabe's wide-eyed wonder had felt pleasant.

Raven was dressed a bit more daringly in a plunging black gown with a narrow skirt and long, gem-studded sleeves that ended in a web of lace at her fingertips. Her costume was complete with a sliver of a red mask across her eyes to match the bright red color on her lips. She wore her hair down long, a sleek waterfall of rich back curls.

"Isn't it customary to wear it up?" I asked.

"Yes," she said. "Your goal is to blend in. Mine is to stand out."

A steamcoach pulled up to the front of Korr's house, and we climbed inside, our gowns rustling.

"Are you supposed to be going to parties if you're just a maid in Korr's house?" I asked.

Raven laughed. "I'm not a maid. The official story is that I'm his ward, visiting from the backwater plains of Aeralis. That way I can be seen at parties, and I can do my work of getting information out of all kinds of desperate, attention-hungry men. But yes, I do pull my weight around the house, if that's what you mean. We all do. Korr let some of the servants go so he could have better control of who sees what goes on in the house, and we all have to pitch in a little."

I found it hard to imagine Korr without a full retinue of servants, but I didn't say that.

The steamcoach rattled as it crossed a bridge of steel and stone. Mist swirled around us, obscuring the view, and a spasm of apprehension gripped my chest. I turned my head and found Raven watching me.

"You're a bit of a puzzle," she said. "You're fierce, but nervous, like a little bird. You act as though you have no fear, but look at you—you're quaking." Her smile turned contemplative as she remembered my moniker. "Bluewing," she said.

Was she mocking me? "When you love someone, you face your fears for them," I said.

I expected a smirk in response, but Raven leaned back as if actually considering my words. "Perhaps so." She lifted one eyebrow. "I wouldn't know."

I chose not to respond. We rode in silence for a few minutes.

"Adam says you owe him a favor," I said quietly.

Raven laughed, low and throaty. "Yes. He helped me out of a situation by pretending to be involved with me. It was rather enjoyable." She observed my expression. "Jealous? I thought you two were no longer speaking."

"We've had a disagreement," I said stiffly.

Raven cleared her throat. "When we reach the party, we'll disembark from the steamcoach together, but separate as soon as we're inside. I do my best work when I'm on my own, and a girl like you wouldn't keep company with a girl like me anyway." She shifted on the seat, crossing her legs and swinging one foot as she spoke. "We can meet again by the coach house at midnight. I suggest you try to find out any information you can, but in all likelihood, you won't. So don't feel too badly about it."

"And you?" I asked, ignoring her suggestion that I was doomed to fail.

"I know who'll talk to me. The man who oversees the camps has a little crush, we'll say. I should have the location of Falcon by midnight."

"Midnight?" I repeated in disbelief.

Her smirk was back. "We can make it eleven if you want to bet on it."

"No," I said. "Just get it as soon as possible. I don't care when."

She leaned back with a smile, as if she'd won an argument. I looked out the window and knit my fingers together in my lap. She annoyed me, but still I hoped desperately that she would succeed. Jonn and Ivy needed her to succeed.

We reached a neighborhood in the shadow of the palace. Ornate buildings of thick stone rose from the mists, topped with towers and clocks and lit by gas lamps. The steamcoach stopped, and Raven motioned for me to follow her out. The steamcoach pulled away as soon as we disembarked, leaving us standing on the mist-steeped steps to the vast house. Raven started up the steps, and I followed her.

Light glimmered on the railings and the branches that edged the walk. A servant stepped forward to take our coats, and we were ushered into a room filled with music and light. I followed Raven and did my best not to gawk at the swirling couples, glittering chandeliers, and tables spread with desserts. We edged through the crowd and reached the far wall. Raven paused beneath a vase almost as tall as she was. She studied my expression. "Overwhelmed?"

"I've seen more impressive sights," I said, thinking of Echlos.

She shrugged and smiled. It was impossible to tell if she thought I was lying. After studying me another moment, she turned toward the dance floor. "Remember," she said over her shoulder. "The coach house at midnight." With that, she vanished into a sea of men and women dressed in velvet and dripping with jewelry.

I stood alone beneath the vase for the space of a few breaths, collecting myself before plunging into the crowd.

Gabe had explained earlier what I'd be looking for, and it hadn't sounded easy. I slipped toward the staircase at the end of the room, skirting a group of giggling young women and men with wine glasses in their hands. The music faded behind me as I headed up the staircase and turned a corner. I padded down a long hallway, counting the doors. Gabe had said it would be the sixth one, with a crest on it.

The music faded, and a dust-drenched silence closed around me. I spotted the door Gabe had described and slipped to it.

The room was dark. I fumbled along the wall for the switch for the gas lamps and didn't find one. My fingers brushed over wallpaper and plaster. The curtains on the windows were open to let in the view of the city, and the faint light from the streetlamps glowed through the rain-studded glass and pooled on the carpet. As my eyes adjusted, I could make out the faint, unyielding shape of bookshelves and the soft curve of a chair. The smooth surface of a desk gleamed, seamed with silvery light around the edges. A fireplace stood in the corner, filled with ashes. A study.

I stepped farther into the room. The floor squeaked under my feet, and I held my breath, but nothing stirred. No one came running down the hall. Reaching into my pocket, I pulled out a box of matches and lit one.

The yellow light flared in the blackness, illuminating one of the bookcases. I knelt before it, scanning the backs of the books, looking for the name Gabe had given me. The book was simply a list of records from three years ago, and I couldn't guess what Gabe needed from it, or why he felt the need for such secrecy that he dared not confide in anyone but me.

The match winked out, burning my fingers. I hissed in pain and lit another, holding it close as my lips moved silently, reading the titles.

Footsteps sounded in the hall, and I dropped the second match and darted toward the window. I managed to squeeze between the wall and one of the curtains before whoever it was entered the room. I heard the soft murmur of voices, and my heart thudded. If anyone looked hard enough, my feet would be visible at the place where the curtain didn't quite reach the floor.

I heard the rasp of a match striking and smelled smoke. They'd lit cigs. They were settling in for a while, whoever they were.

"Nothing I like better than a few hours of silence. These days, it's hard to come by," a male voice said with a weary groan.

A few hours? Panic filled me. I had to meet Raven at midnight.

"Aye, especially with these whispers of Restorationists..." a second voice said, also male. This one sounded infinitely weary.

I stilled. My heart thumped at the mention of Restorationists. What did they know?

"I've heard talk that they have a worm in their midst." A chuckle, low and hard. "If that's true, they won't last long."

A worm? As in, a spy?

Coldness filled me, spreading from my chest to my extremities.

"Are those *matches* on the rug?" the first voice demanded. "If the maids have been smoking in my study again... I smell smoke! My books!"

There was a pause.

"Nothing is burned, at least."

"I ought to let them go, all of them. Fools. Look around, see if they dropped any other matches."

I shut my eyes and tried not to breathe, lest it make the curtain flutter.

"Now, now. Calm yourself. Have a cig."

"I have a particularly fine new brand from the south."

A drawer opened and shut.

"Wait," a voice said. "The box is in the library. It's just down the hall. Accompany me?"

As soon as the footsteps faded, I slipped from behind the curtain and ran for the door. My heart thudded against my ribs and my vision spun. I reached the doorway and entered the hall.

The voices were a murmur, growing louder again.

I fled down the hall before they returned and stopped around the corner. I pressed my back to the wall. My hands trembled. Below, the gowns of the dancing women shimmered in the light of the chandeliers. Music wafted upward, dulling the sound of my pounding pulse that thundered in my ears. I stepped to the rail and looked over, and my breath snagged. A lean, dark-haired man stood by the door, wearing a dark coat and carrying a hat in his hands.

Adam?

As I watched, a servant took his coat and hat. The man looked up as if he felt my attention, and our eyes met.

It *was* Adam.

He froze at the sight of me, his eyes darkening and his body going still as the rest of the crowd flowed around him. His mouth turned down, and he started for the stairs.

I descended to meet him, because I wasn't running or hiding. I wanted that to be clear. We met halfway, he on the step below me. My chin rose a little so I could look him in the eye. His hand curled around my arm, and he leaned in. He smelled of soap and pine. A shiver prickled my arms.

"What are you doing here?" he murmured in my ear. There was an edge to his tone.

I drew back and gazed into his eyes, unwavering in my expression. "I could ask you the same question."

Exasperation flitted across his face. "Lia," he said, as if simply saying my name in that irritated voice told me anything.

Guests glanced at us curiously.

The words I'd overheard about spies among the Restorationists still echoed in my ears. I struggled to breathe calmly, to lift my chin as if I knew nothing new. "I hear this house has a beautiful conservatory," I said. "Shall we find it?"

Adam sighed and offered me his arm. I slid my fingers over his jacket, feeling the warm muscle beneath, and something in my stomach clenched. I let him lead me through the crowd toward a pair of arched doors. We passed a fountain of lemonade and mounds of fruit spread across half a dozen tables. The music grew louder, drowning out the titter of nervous laughter and the hum of voices eager to share the latest news and gossip.

Servants drew the doors to the conservatory open for us. Beyond, a glass ceiling glittered in the gaslight. Branches hung low over the path, obscuring us as we strolled arm in arm like any couple in love. Ferns rustled at my feet, and the air smelled like sweet earth and honeysuckle. It reminded me of the greenhouse in the Frost, the one we'd found when we were starving, and a fierce ache filled me at the memory.

When we'd walked far enough into the conservatory to be alone and out of earshot, Adam dropped my arm and whirled on me. "What are you doing here?"

"Raven is obtaining the information about Borde. I wanted to keep an eye on her." I omitted the part about my errand for Gabe, because that was not my secret to tell.

"Raven is seasoned at her job. She is used to navigating these sorts of parties. You, on the other hand—"

"Contrary to what everyone seems to think, I'm not a bumbling idiot," I snapped. "Just because I'm not surrounded by snow doesn't mean I'm incapable of handling myself. I've been here before, and I managed fine."

"I know," he said. The admission was soft, almost gentle. I looked at him, but I couldn't read the expression in his eyes.

We were silent. Faintly, I heard the music of the party swelling louder as the doors to the conservatory opened and closed behind us. Half of Adam's mouth lifted in a grimace as he scanned my dress, my jewelry, my hair.

"You do look the part," he said. He admitted it as if the words pained him, as if he spoke them against his better judgment or even against his will. His jaw flexed, and he looked away. "Like a true Aeralian. Like you belong here."

I didn't know what to say. His words unlocked something inside me that felt bruised and fragile. The air around us was prickly, fraught with thorny unspoken hurts and tangled intentions. I fumbled for words, any words, as I smoothed both hands over the fabric. "It's Ann's."

"Ann has impeccable taste," he said quietly, "but I prefer you in your blue cloak."

This was Adam, my Adam, the same man who had taught me to navigate the Frost and who'd patiently let me sort out my myriad feelings before. Now there was coldness between us. He was looking at me with such sadness now, such confusion.

My throat tightened.

The doors opened, and more guests streamed into the conservatory, breaking the moment. A few of the newcomers glanced our way, and as a new set of music began in the other room, Adam offered me his hands.

"We should dance," he said quietly, reluctantly. "It will make us less conspicuous."

I put my fingers in his, and he drew me close as we began to move in a slow waltz. His breath was soft against my cheek; his hands were warm on my back and against my wrist. I didn't dare look at his eyes. Mine might betray me.

"Why are you here tonight?" I asked to put words in the air between us. "You never told me."

"Thorns mission," he said.

"Raven's mission?"

He didn't reply, and I remembered that I no longer had any right to that kind of information now that I was out of the Thorns.

An ache started in my chest. Had I made the right decision?

Of course I had. I'd made the only decision I could have made. I'd chosen my family, and that was not a mistake. It would never be a mistake.

Adam's fingers found my chin and lifted it so my eyes met his.

"I know it's complicated between us," he said. "But we need to talk about it."

I pulled away slightly. "Then talk."

He shook his head. "Not now. I have the mission. Soon, though."

I felt no desire to urge him to talk about how he wanted nothing to do with me, how I was reckless and irresponsible, how he was a Thorns agent and I was not, and that was what really mattered. I took a deep breath and let it hiss between my teeth as I nodded anyway. I owed him that much.

The song ended, and Adam released me. Cold air rushed over my skin where he'd been touching me, and I wrapped my arms around myself for warmth.

"I have to meet Raven at midnight," I said.

He pushed back his sleeve to reveal a Farther device—a tiny clock strapped to his wrist, ticking and purring as its gears spun. "You have a little time." He hesitated. "But I should go."

I watched as he headed back into the main ballroom, and my whole world was pain as he stepped out of sight and into the crowd.

~

Raven met me as the clock tower was striking midnight. Heat flushed her cheeks, and she was breathing hard. Her eyes sparkled as if she'd just done something she found delightful.

"Did you get it?" I demanded.

"Patience," she crooned, brushing past me for the steamcoach. "I'll tell you inside."

I dragged up my heavy skirts and followed her inside. My stomach twisted with impatience as she sprawled across one of the seats and propped her feet on the other. Raven tipped her head up at me, smirking at my obvious distress.

"Calm yourself, Frostie," she said. "I have your information."

I sighed with relief.

"It was easy enough to get," she continued, "when I asked him sweetly. It's a good thing you didn't take that bet. I got it out of him by ten thirty. All it took was a few smiles."

I didn't really want to know how she had to flirt with him to get the location of Borde. I shook my head at the impending story and asked, "Well?"

She reached into the bodice of her dress and pulled out a scrap of paper. "I wrote it out for you."

I snatched the paper, still warm from her skin, and smoothed it in my lap. Raven's neat penmanship covered the bit of page, giving both the name and location of the camp.

We were one step closer.

FIFTEEN

GABE MET ME in the hall outside my room.

"Did you find it?" he whispered, peering past me to make sure we were alone as he spoke.

"I didn't have a chance to finish looking." I explained how I'd almost been discovered in the process of searching, and Gabe's expression turned to pure horror.

"I didn't realize you would be in danger." He paused, his hands curling into fists as he spoke half to himself. "It was wrong of me to ask you to find it. I put you in danger."

"I managed to slip out unseen," I said. "But there's something else you should know. The men in the room were talking while I hid. They spoke of the Restorationists. They said there's a spy in our midst."

Gabe shut his eyes. "I knew it."

"You knew there was a spy? And what's in this book of records?"

Gabe licked his lower lip and glanced around again. "I must tell you in private."

I pushed off the wall and opened the door to my room. He hesitated, and I gestured for him to follow me inside. He pinked slightly but didn't argue. Once we were inside, Gabe lingered near the door, his hands restless while I lit a gas lamp.

"Tell me," I said, turning back to him. "Please."

"The book of records holds the name of the person who betrayed my family to the Dictator. Gave him access to the palace, told his men our comings and goings."

I pulled off my coat and threw it over a chair. I waited for him to continue.

Gabe's eyebrows pinched together as he spoke the next words. "I told you before that someone betrayed my family. I don't know who, but I'm afraid... Clara's family worked for the royal family. They had access."

"You think her family betrayed yours to the Dictator?"

His throat convulsed as he swallowed. "I just need to know for sure it isn't her." He stopped. "And as you heard tonight, someone is leaking information."

"You think it's Claire?"

"I—no! Well. I just want to be sure." Frustration and fear crossed his face.

"You love her," I observed, and immediately regretted it. It seemed like a stupid thing to say, and I didn't know why I had.

Gabe blinked. "Of course I do. She's my friend."

That wasn't what I'd meant, but I said nothing else. I wasn't Ann; I didn't prod people to talk endlessly about their feelings, and I certainly wasn't comfortable having this discussion with him. An uncomfortable emotion that felt like loss or jealousy or sadness, or all three bundled up together, simmered in my stomach. I stuffed it away to ponder later and focused on the conversation at hand while Gabe paced restlessly, his arms crossed tightly and his face pinched in a scowl.

"So you want to get this book of records to see if she's the one who betrayed you all those years ago?"

"The name of the informants should be listed. As I'm a traitor to the crown—and supposed to be dead—it's hardly a great secret that must be guarded with too much care. It's simply something no one would remember, because why does it matter to them?"

"Surely Korr would care."

Gabe looked ill.

"But you don't want him to know she's betraying you?"

He groaned. "I have to give her a chance to explain herself. If Korr found out, he'd have her killed. He has no mercy for traitors, not now."

"Do we have another chance to retrieve the book?" I asked.

Gabe's shoulders sagged. "Not that I know of. Entry to that house is rarely granted. The party was a rare occasion. But thank you. I appreciate your concern for my feelings."

"Gabe," I said, annoyed now. "If someone is betraying you, they need to be found before someone gets hurt. You, or if you don't care about your own safety, Ann." Or Adam, my mind whispered traitorously.

"Please," he said. "I need to find out if it's true. If Korr knew what I suspect—even if I'm wrong—she'll be dispatched anyway. Korr already doesn't trust her. I don't need to give him another reason not to."

Dispatched. A shudder ran through me.

This was a complication I didn't need. I needed to find Borde and his device and return to the Frost. However, the expression in Gabe's eyes stirred me. It was the look of a wild thing trapped in a cage, desperate and terrified. It mirrored the way I felt whenever I remembered Jonn's listless body beneath the quilt, the way I'd felt when I'd seen Ivy in Gordon's clutches.

"What do you propose we do?" I asked, the words coming out like a sigh.

His panic thawed a little. "Thank you. I'm not sure, but thank you."

Somewhere, a clock struck one in the morning. It was late.

"I'll keep thinking of a plan," Gabe said. He slipped from the room, leaving me alone.

I bathed, undressed, and tried to sleep, but I stared at the ceiling for a long time before unconsciousness claimed me.

~

I met Korr in his study the next morning. Raven joined us, much to my chagrin.

"I see you've found the location of your friend," Korr said, looking from me to Raven. "Thanks to my resources."

"She did it on her own time," I said sharply.

Raven smirked at us both and leaned back against the desk, arching her neck and exposing the line of her collarbone. A necklace consisting of a single pearl on a silver strand glimmered there, like a frozen teardrop. "Don't fight. There's enough of me for everyone."

Korr gave her a look that said he found her less than amusing. She returned it with one that said she was only playing.

I had no patience for their cat-and-mouse games of attraction and power. "When are we rescuing Falcon?"

The door to the study opened, and Adam stepped inside, his coat on his arm and his clothing damp from the outside. He tossed his coat over a chair, crossed his arms, and leaned against the wall. Our eyes met, and I was the one to look away first.

"Now that we're all here," Korr said, "we can discuss the plan. According to the information Nettie here provided, he's being held in the camp on the far side of the city, called Blackmouth."

Raven's eyes narrowed into slits at the use of her real name, and she made a small sound of derisive outrage. Korr ignored her.

"What has to be done to extract him?"

"I'll have to acquire passes to get you in. Brewer will accompany us, and Nettie is coming along to serve as a distraction," Korr said.

"Us?" I asked.

"Of course I'm coming," he said. "What else will stop you from taking the man and running straight for the Frost with no regard for our agreement?"

My heart thumped hard against my ribs. I didn't answer. Ivy's face floated before my eyes. We were running out of time, and Korr was only making everything more complicated by refusing to trust me.

"Fine," I gritted out. There was no time, and arguing would only waste what little we didn't have. "When can we leave?"

"Patience," Korr said in a tone that made my blood boil. "This afternoon. We need time to assemble your costumes."

"Costumes?"

He smiled.

~

Blackmouth was as ugly as its name suggested. A snarl of metal fences ringed a collection of stone buildings, and the sight of them reminded me of the Farther occupation of the Frost. Scum scudded the sides and roofs of the buildings, and seaweed clung to the bottoms of the fences where they bit into the sandy shore. The river Black surged past the dock that led to the camp, and the frothy water was thick with debris and garbage from the city. The stench of sewage filled the air.

Our cart rattled as it crossed the wooden bridge that led to the camp. Raven sat beside Korr in the front of the cart, and Adam and I crouched in the back. Adam's eyes met mine and slid away to focus on the camp ahead. His chest rose and fell with even breaths, but his hands were still against the sides of the wagon, betraying his tension. I clung to the side as the wheels shuddered and bounced over the uneven planks.

"As you can see, these camps were constructed rather hastily," Korr murmured under his breath. "To deal with the influx of dissenters and traitors to the new ruler." His voice was sharp with disgust even though it was muffled by his mask.

We were disguised as a food delivery wagon. We all wore masks designed to help visitors cope with the eye-watering smell of the river and the camp, and our clothes were plain gray and brown with boots and gloves. Adam and I both had caps to cover our hair. Korr wore a beard, and a false scar marred his cheek. Raven had donned a patched dress, and her hair was dirty, but she still looked stunning.

Anxiety rioted in my blood as the camp grew closer. I adjusted my mask and shifted my weight. My legs were falling asleep. I straightened them, flexing my ankles and toes in an effort to limber them.

"We'll be fine," Adam said, for my ears alone.

I looked at him. He was still gazing at the camp, but I felt his attention on me all the same. One side of his mouth quirked in the barest smile.

"This is nothing you haven't done before," he said, and the memory of the day Korr and I had rescued him from an Aeralian prison filled my mind. I'd kissed him. A flush swept over me as I remembered the way it had felt to hold him. Now he sat only a few feet from me, but he might as well be back in the Frost for the gulf of emotional distance between us.

I pulled my mind back to the present as the wagon stopped before the gate to the camp. Soldiers approached, their guns slung low and their mouths slack. They were bored. I breathed in and out, and the sound hissed through my mask. On the seat ahead of me, Raven shifted and gave the men a sideways glance. They both looked at her with idle interest and a glimmer of curiosity. They ignored Adam and me.

Korr handed one of the guards papers that granted us passage—papers he'd forged earlier. The guard scrutinized them and then waved us through.

Adam turned his head and flicked one eyebrow up at me.

Success.

Mud squished beneath the wheels of the wagon as we entered the camp. Rows of huts stretched out toward the water. Rivulets of dirty liquid streamed through the paths between them. In the distance, men and women stood up to their knees in the river, cutting reeds and tying them into bundles.

In the camps, Korr had explained, the prisoners worked all day long performing hard labor. At Blackmouth, they picked reeds from the riverbed and gathered them into bundles to be dried. Then, the bundles were gathered into piles and burned. The futility of the work was part of the torture.

Korr stopped the wagon before the kitchen—a long, low building of stone surrounded by troughs. My eyes widened as I realized the prisoners were fed from the troughs. Anger burned in the pit of my stomach.

Adam touched my wrist, signaling for me to follow him, and we leaped down from the cart. Korr stepped down into the mud, muttering curses as his boots sank into the filth. He nodded at us, and we lifted the cartons of food scraps from the back of the cart and began to carry them toward the kitchen. We set them inside on a grimy brick floor and returned for the rest. The hairs on my neck prickled with apprehension as we worked. A quick glance over my shoulder confirmed that the guards were still watching us.

"Stay here," Korr said to Raven, speaking loud enough that his voice carried across the yard. "I don't want you wandering around. This place is dangerous."

"It smells," she protested. "Can't I come with you?"

They began to bicker while Adam and I slipped around the side of the kitchen. Once out of sight of the guards, we walked briskly for the warden's office.

The warden sat hunched over his desk, eating a slice of dry-looking cake. I wondered how he could eat with the stench of the camp in his nose. When we entered, he straightened and wiped his mouth with the back of his hand. "Yes?"

"We need a few off-duty workers to help us unload our cart," Adam said. He paused. "Is that pecan?"

"Walnut," the warden said, noting Adam's interest and taking another bite with a malicious smile. He licked the crumbs from his lips.

As Adam distracted the warden with a conversation about cake, I scanned the wall behind him. It was covered in the names and numbers of the prisoners, along with marks to indicate their punishments and privileges. My eyes fell on the name I sought.

Falcon.

He was prisoner number 650. My heart pounded, and I stepped on Adam's foot lightly, the signal that I'd found what we needed.

As soon as we'd exited the building, we darted around the side and out of sight of any guards. We pulled off our masks and caps and dropped them behind a barrel. I rubbed a little dirt on my face, and Adam brushed mud across his neck. In our plain garments and without our masks and caps, we looked more like the prisoners—as long as no one noticed how well fed we were.

"Number 650," I said, and Adam nodded. We set off toward the river.

The camp was divided into rows, and it was split in half between men and women prisoners, Korr had explained. The higher numbers were at the back, nearest the river. The prisoner's numbers were posted outside the doors of the huts.

Water from puddles splashed our ankles and mud splattered the legs of our clothes as we slipped around corners and dodged guards on patrol, crossing the camp one row at a time. We weren't alone. Prisoners squatted outside of the huts, urinated in alleyways, and wandered past in a daze. They worked in rotations, and if we were fortunate, Falcon would be in his hut. Nobody spared us more than a glance as we passed. They seemed too weary to care.

I spotted 650 and pointed. "There."

A hand seized my shoulder and spun me around. A guard with drooping lids and a cruel sneer glared down at me. "I thought I told you to bring me a drink from the guardhouse."

My heart thudded against my ribs. "You must be mistaken."

"'You must be mistaken,'" he repeated, mocking me. "What is this, a tea party? I'm not mistaken. It was you. Where's my drink?"

"It wasn't me," I insisted.

He slapped me hard across the face. I staggered back, tasting blood, and Adam stepped in front of me with a sound of protest.

"Hey—"

The guard punched him hard enough to drop him to his knees. When Adam raised his head, the guard hit him again.

"Stop," I shouted, but the guard ignored me. He lifted his fist to strike again.

A splash in the river snagged his attention. He paused. In the distance, two prisoners went down together in a flail of arms and legs. They leaped up again, circling each other among the reeds with their fists up as the other prisoners scattered. The guard muttered under his breath. He reached down to his belt for his whip.

"Let this be a lesson. Don't forget again," the guard snarled at me, and set off for the river.

Adam got to his feet. The right side of his face was already swelling.

"Are you all right?" I asked Adam as soon as the guard had vanished.

He ran a hand over his face and grimaced. "I'll live. You?"

"He isn't the first Aeralian that's ever slapped me."

Adam's eyes sparked with anger. "He will be the last, I swear it."

I looked to the hut. "We need to hurry before he comes back."

The inside of the hut was shadowy and smelled like rotting fish. Four bunk beds built with splintered boards lined the walls. A sleeping figure occupied one, but he was too young to be Borde.

Footsteps sounded in the doorway. Adam pressed himself against the wall, and I whirled, looking for a place to hide as a figure entered. It was an old man, but not Borde. He spotted me before I could move.

"Who are you?" he asked, wary but not alarmed. He hadn't seen Adam, who was crouched against the wall and ready to spring if necessary.

"I'm looking for prisoner number 650," I said, ignoring his question.

The man grunted and gestured at the sleeping figure. "He's right there."

I turned. "That isn't him."

The man snorted. "It's him. He stepped past me for another bunk and rolled into it. Within seconds, he was asleep.

Adam stepped from the shadows and looked from me to the first man, the one who had been identified as 650. I stepped closer and peered at his face even as disappointment surged through me.

Had another man named Falcon been arrested? Was this all for nothing?

Shock sizzled through me as the man shifted and I caught a glimpse of his features. His hair, his eyes, his nose, his mouth were all as familiar to me as my own face.

The man sleeping on the bunk before me looked exactly like Jonn.

SIXTEEN

MY GASP WAS loud enough to wake the prisoner. He bolted upright, squinting at us both in the near-darkness as he raised his fists.

"Who are you?"

I tried to speak, but no sound emerged from my mouth. I looked at Adam wildly—did he see it, too? Was I hallucinating? Was I losing my mind in the tension of the moment?

"Who are you?" the prisoner repeated angrily. "I don't have any extra money or food."

Adam touched my arm to show that he recognized the resemblance, too. He nodded at me, urging me to speak.

"Please," I said, turning back to the man. "We must talk to you."

He was older than Jonn by at least twenty years, with streaks of gray hair running along the sides of his head and lines around the corners of his eyes and mouth, but there was no mistaking the astonishing similarity. I thought of my mother's letter.

There is something you need to know, something I've not yet had the courage to tell you.

My knees buckled.

"Aaron?" I whispered, and the word burned on my lips as I spoke it.

It was my father's name. The prisoner's eyes widened slightly at the name before closing almost into slits. He got to his feet.

"What do you want? Why did you call me that?"

Confusion spiraled through me, but there wasn't time to think. I held up both hands to calm him. "We're here to help you."

He stumbled back. "Eloisa?"

Eloisa. My mother's name. My heart thudded against my ribs. My knees trembled. My hands were numb.

"No. It's Lia," I managed.

"Lia?" He was confused.

"Camilla," I said. It was the name I'd been given at birth, the name I'd been called as a baby.

He went still at my name, and I took a shuddering breath. He knew my mother's name. He knew my name. He looked just like Jonn.

There is something you need to know, my mother had written.

I couldn't think, couldn't move. I was paralyzed by the possibility smoldering painfully in my mind like a live coal, and all the emotional upheaval facing it would cause.

"We don't have time," Adam murmured in my ear as he touched my elbow, bringing me back to the present. "Later." His voice was sympathetic, but the urgency in it roused me back to what must be done.

"Listen," I said to the man I'd called Aaron, speaking fast. "We came to find Falcon. Where is he?"

The prisoner lowered his voice and looked at Adam. "Who is he?"

"He can be trusted," I said. "Please. We have to hurry. Where's Falcon?"

"I'm Falcon," the prisoner said angrily.

I tried again. "Where is Meridus Borde?"

The man's eyes hardened. He shook his head. "There's no one by that name here." He turned, and I caught a glimpse of the tattoo on his arm—650. He hadn't been lying about that.

Adam touched my arm. "Lia. We're out of time."

Panic filled me. We hadn't found Borde. Instead here stood a stranger who knew my mother's name and looked exactly like my brother.

"Come with us," I blurted. "We'll smuggle you out of here."

"What? How?"

"No time to explain. You'll have to trust me. Do you trust me?"

The prisoner nodded. He was gazing at my face, a dazed expression on his own.

"Stay close, follow us, and do what we say," I said. "Your life will depend on it. Understand?"

"I understand."

"We've got to get back to the kitchen," I told him. "We've got a cart there. My friends are waiting for us."

"The guards—"

"There's a secret compartment under the cart," I explained.

He licked his lips and nodded after a pause. His eyes shifted from me to Adam. "Who's he?" he asked again.

"Someone you can trust," I said firmly. I felt Adam's eyes on me when I said it, but I didn't look at him. I kept my gaze fixed on the prisoner.

"I suppose I don't have much choice," he said.

Adam and I exchanged a glance. We darted across the alley to the adjacent row of huts with the prisoner at our heels. We moved from row to row, avoiding the patrolling guards as we slipped toward the front of the camp where Korr, Raven, and the cart waited. When we reached the place where Adam and I had stored our masks and caps, I stopped to retrieve them. After slipping them back on, we continued toward the kitchen.

Raven's voice carried clearly through the stillness. Korr's answering rumble simmered with impatience. They were arguing.

I turned to face the prisoner when we reached the corner of the kitchen that was closest to the yard. "We'll go out first," I said. "Keep your eyes on me. I'll motion for you to come when the guards are occupied, and you'll go under the cart. There is a compartment there that you can climb into and lie flat inside of. Remain there until we tell you to come out, and don't make a sound."

He nodded.

Adam and I rounded the corner together. Korr and Raven stood in the middle of the yard, face-to-face, arguing. Raven had both hands on her hips. Korr's arms were crossed, and he hissed commands at her. I couldn't make out their words, but it seemed they were disagreeing about whether she should be allowed to speak to the soldiers.

The guards were watching the fight with undisguised enjoyment. They looked at us as we appeared, and then their gazes returned to the more interesting argument as Raven's tone rose to a squeal.

Every muscle in my body was screaming with tension. I didn't take my eyes off the guards as I approached the cart. I motioned to the prisoner behind my back. I heard the squish of his feet in the mud, and then the creak of the cart as he slipped beneath it and climbed into the compartment we'd fixed there earlier in the day.

One of the guards straightened and approached.

"You there," he said to me.

I couldn't breathe. Korr and Raven fell silent. They turned. Korr's face was impassive, but Raven's eyes were wide with sudden fear as the guard stopped before the cart.

"What took you so long?" he asked me.

My throat was dry. My lips were numb. "I...we...we had to—"

The guard laughed, interrupting my explanation. He spat in the mud. "Next time, do it again. These two are more entertaining than a night at the theater."

I sagged against the cart as he returned to his post. Adam and I climbed into the back of the cart, while Korr and Raven situated themselves on the driver's bench, still bickering. I didn't relax until we'd passed through the gate and crossed the bridge to Astralux.

~

When we reached the end of the industrial side of the city, Korr pulled the cart into an alley and jumped down from the driver's seat.

"Hurry," he barked. "We don't have much time before nightfall, and this section of the city has a curfew."

A steamcoach pulled up in the street with a wheeze of mist. The coach was plain gray, not Korr's usual gleaming black one.

I crouched on the ground beside the cart and peered at the underside. "Come out. We have to change vehicles now."

The prisoner's hands appeared, then his head. He emerged from the compartment with a groan, tumbling to the ground and scrambling up immediately, as if he expected one of us to grab him and put a gun to his head.

"Are you all right?" Adam asked him quietly.

One corner of the prisoner's mouth slid up in a grimace of a smile. "I'm alive." He scanned our faces until he found mine, and he stared at me. "Lia," he said, testing the word on his tongue. He spoke with a mixture of disbelief and awe.

Raven and Korr both looked at him, their attention snagged by the tone of his voice.

My throat squeezed as I saw him again in the light of day. The tilt of his nose, the squint of his eyes, the way his hair swirled over his left ear—it was all Jonn.

Who was this man who answered to my father's name? Who looked like a Weaver?

The prisoner looked at Korr and Raven with open curiosity.

"Who are you?" he asked Korr, his voice thorny with hostility. "You look familiar. You have the stink of nobility."

The skin around Korr's eyes tightened. "I'll ask the questions," he said. "You're in our debt. Remember that."

Aaron crossed his arms and straightened his stance. Tension filled the air. I swallowed. I hadn't thought we might be dealing with an uncooperative rescuee. I stepped forward and put a hand on his arm.

"Let's get going, shall we?" I said.

"Yes," Korr said with a flick of his eyebrow. "Unless you want us to leave you here? You'll be found within hours, I can assure you."

"And if I come with you?" the prisoner demanded.

"We're not going to hurt you," Korr said. "At least not as long as you behave yourself. We have need of you—"

"You can trust us," I said, cutting off Korr's less-than-reassuring reassurance. I didn't want Korr spilling our plans to this prisoner, not when he wasn't the real man we needed. Korr couldn't know that yet, not until I'd figured out what to do.

The prisoner looked at the waiting coach, then back at me. Slowly, he uncrossed his arms and nodded, and I breathed out with relief.

"Let's get out of here."

~

Adam and I waited together in the library as the prisoner bathed and ate. Adam sat in the window, one leg drawn up to his chest, his chin cupped in his hand as he stared at the darkened street below. I paced, trying to make sense of everything and failing. The words of my mother's letter circled in my mind like birds. In my hand, clenched between my fingers and my palm, was the tattered bit of letter she'd left me. I had the words memorized by now, but I read them again anyway. This man. His appearance. The letter. And my mission. Borde. It was all too much. I shut my eyes and took a deep breath.

"Where is Borde?" I muttered. "And why did the prisoner take his name?" I opened my eyes and stared at nothing, trying to think.

Adam looked at me but didn't say anything.

"Do you think...do you think he's dead?" Horror pierced me as I spoke the words.

"Don't make assumptions yet," Adam said. He rose and stood in front of me, blocking me from pacing another circuit around the room. "Let's talk to him first."

My eyes burned. "Why does he look like Jonn?"

Adam said nothing, but his eyes softened. He reached out and touched my cheek with one hand, and I let him. The brush of his fingers sent a chill over my skin, but it was oddly comforting.

A knock at the door startled us.

I turned away from Adam to open it. The prisoner stood in the hall, flanked by two of Korr's men. His hair was damp and he smelled like soap. He wore a fresh set of clothing that was slightly too large for his emaciated frame.

I nodded at the guards, and they left us. "Come in," I said to him.

"So, I take it I'm still a prisoner?" he observed, glancing behind him at the retreating men.

"Korr is taking no chances at the moment. Don't take it to mean more than what it does. He is a cautious man."

"Korr," he said. "I know that name." His forehead wrinkled as he thought, and he blanched. "He's one of the favorites of the Dictator."

"He's a Restorationist," I said. "He can be"—I winced at the word—"trusted. At least, he is not our direct enemy."

The prisoner nodded at the word *Restorationist*. I wondered how much he knew about them, but didn't ask. There were more pressing questions on my mind.

"Where's Borde?"

The prisoner's eyes darted from me to Adam. "Tell me who he is first," he demanded.

"Adam Brewer," Adam said, introducing himself. "I'm a Frost dweller like Lia. Like you."

"Frost dweller," the prisoner said. "I no longer take that title."

Silence swept over the room, heavy with unspoken things.

So he was from the Frost.

I took a deep breath. "In the prison, you called me Eloisa."

"Yes." He paused. "My wife's name. And you called me Aaron, which is mine."

My stomach fell like a stone. I held out the remnant of my mother's letter, and he took the letter as if it were a baby bird, impossibly fragile but somehow infinitely precious, too. His lips moved as he read the words, but he didn't make a sound. I waited. His eyes reddened, and his posture slowly slumped as he absorbed the words. Finally, he raised his gaze to mine.

"You're my daughter," he said.

I shivered at the admission uttered so plainly.

"How?"

"I fell through the gate," he said. "I discovered how to activate it, and it ate me alive. I ended up in the past, and I was trapped there."

"I grew up with a father named Aaron," I said.

He rubbed his forehead. "The fugitive. He must have assumed my identity. Eloisa was pregnant at the time. We were not well known in the village; my face was not familiar to most. She would need a provider, and no one would have known. It would be the most sensible thing for them to do." He laughed shakily, bitterly. "How brilliant of them."

I exhaled. This was insane. The man I'd called da was really an Aeralian fugitive?

"You've been back in the Frost for months now," I said. "Yet you never came to find us. Why didn't you return to the Frost when you came back with Borde?"

Aaron didn't respond for a long moment. He rubbed his neck with one hand before answering. "Meridus needed my help. And I..." He shook his head and looked away at the windowpanes and the street beyond. "I'd been gone a long time. That life was like a dream to me. Perhaps you were all better off with me staying out of it."

The words ripped through me like bullets.

Perhaps you were all better off with me staying out of it.

Perhaps we were. I breathed in and out, sorting words in my head, suppressing insults and accusations on my tongue.

Aaron cleared his throat. "How is Eloisa?"

"She's dead." I said it flatly. The words landed between us like rocks. Aaron's jaw twitched. He went to the window and sank into the place where Adam had been sitting earlier. Putting his face in his hands, he asked, "How?"

"We thought it was Watchers at first," I said. The words came out harsh. "But she was shot by a fellow villager, a traitor who was working with the Mayor to help the Aeralians."

"You don't call them Farthers," he observed numbly, staring into space.

"Not much, at least not anymore," I said. They weren't so far from me anymore, not since I'd learned to love one of them, not since I'd worked alongside them.

"And your brother?"

"Jonn..." I hesitated. "He has the Sickness."

Aaron's shoulders stiffened. He lifted his head. "The Sickness? How?"

"I brought it back with me at his request after I passed through the Echlos gate to the Frost's past. Surely Borde told you."

Aaron gave no indication one way or the other that I was right in my assumption. He stared at the window without appearing to see it. "And is he...is he dying?"

"Yes."

Aaron looked stricken.

"There's more." I took a deep breath. "You are perhaps familiar with a man called Gordon."

Aaron scowled but didn't reply.

"He followed you and Borde into the Frost, but he says he lost you there. He wants something."

"He'll never get it," Aaron said sharply.

"He infected my sister, Ivy."

Aaron blinked. "Ivy?"

"My sister. Your other daughter, the one Ma was expecting when you disappeared. You never met her, and if I don't get that device Borde is here to find, she'll die, along with Jonn. But Gordon says he has a cure, and he'll give it to me if I give him the device."

Aaron was white-faced. He said nothing.

"We need to find Borde," I bit out. "Afterward, you can go on with your life. You don't have to come back to us. We never even knew you were missing, so don't feel any obligation, because you have none."

Adam cleared his throat. I'd forgotten he was there. He touched my arm, giving me strength through his fingertips. I leaned into him, and his hands slid down my arms, a silent reminder of his support.

"Where is Borde?" I said.

Aaron stared off into space. His hands moved restlessly. "I don't know."

"You took his name," I snapped. "You must know something."

"They came for him," he said. "We were together, staying in the city, when the soldiers came to arrest him. He'd gone out to buy food, and I was in the house alone. They arrested me instead, without asking any questions, and when they interrogated me, I told them I was Falcon."

"You gave yourself in his place?"

"They weren't going to let me go. At least by giving them his name, they would stop looking for him."

"Can you give us any ideas of where Borde might be now?" Adam asked.

"I imagine he fled once he heard of my arrest. He's probably in hiding under a different name now."

"You think he's in the city?"

"When I was arrested, we had not yet found what we'd come for." Aaron paused. "Yes, I think he's in the city still."

"Where?" I demanded.

"I don't know," he said. He was turning a pale color, and sweat began to drip down his face. "I haven't the faintest idea."

"Lia," Adam said, laying a hand on my arm. "Perhaps he needs more rest."

"There isn't time—"

"A short break," Adam said. He looked at Aaron. "The guards will escort you back to your room and bring you a little food."

The door slammed shut behind Aaron, leaving Adam and me alone. Despair rushed over me in a black flood.

SEVENTEEN

"WHAT ARE WE going to do?" Panic closed my throat. Without Borde, I wouldn't have the device, and without the device, I wouldn't have the cure for the Sickness. Jonn and Ivy would die.

"There's still time," Adam said.

"And if Korr discovers that the man we rescued isn't the man who can fix the gate for him?" I shut my eyes in despair.

"Lia." Adam touched my elbows gently, bringing me back to the moment. I opened my eyes and looked at him. "We'll figure something out."

I ground my teeth and turned away. "We need to search the city. Return to what we were doing before. We have to find him."

"And your father?"

I whirled on him. "Don't call him my father again."

Adam winced. "I apologize. I won't."

I sighed. "Gabe had a contact that we spoke to a few days ago. Perhaps he knows something. In the meantime, we should probably speak to...to Aaron again, see what he knows."

Adam nodded.

I thought of Jonn again, and my throat squeezed. "We're running out of time."

"We'll find him."

But I wasn't so sure.

Aaron returned a short while later, this time accompanied by Gabe. He faced me and crossed his arms, as if readying himself for the interrogation he knew was coming.

"If we can't find Borde, then I need the device he came here to find." I said. "Where is it?"

Aaron tipped his head to the side and stared at me. "What did your mother tell you about me? How did you know who I was?"

I bit my lip. We didn't have time for this. "You look like Jonn," I admitted.

His eyelids flickered.

I wet my lips. Maybe talking about this would make him more cooperative. "We had a father," I said.

"The fugitive."

"Yes. I never doubted for a moment that he was the real Aaron Weaver until I saw you in the death camp. I didn't know the truth until today."

We were silent.

"You look so much like her," he said. Every syllable he spoke ached with something heavy and dark—regret?

It galled me to beg, but I had no choice. "Please," I said. "If we don't find Borde, my sister will die. My brother will die. Your *son and daughter* will die."

"They're not mine anymore," Aaron said. "You said it yourself. You already have a father."

"Had," I said. "He's dead, too."

Aaron looked down at his hands, his face expressionless. "I'm sorry to hear that."

Pain filled me, but I pushed it aside and continued. "The point is, you are our only connection to Borde right now. Korr in particular isn't going to feel any remorse about forcing answers out of you. I don't want it to come to that, but..." I let the implication hang in the air.

Gabe spoke up. "You have a tremendous amount of loyalty for Borde."

Aaron rubbed the back of his neck. "He was good to me. Helped me...cared for me. He was loyal to me. I'm not about to scorn that so easily."

I bit my lip to hold in words about his loyalty to his family. "We aren't going to hurt him. Borde is my friend. I knew him in his time. Perhaps we can help him."

Aaron snorted. "You have your own agenda. Don't try to pretend you care about ours."

Helpless rage surged in me. I stepped into the hall and took a few deep breaths. Gabe and Adam followed me.

"I don't know how much longer I can keep Korr happy with the explanation that he's exhausted from his rescue," Gabe said. "My brother is going to want answers about the gate soon."

"And time is rapidly passing," I muttered, thinking of the capsule in my sister.

"We need to return to Ferris and see if he's found anything," Gabe said. "Lia?"

"Yes," I agreed. "Today, if possible. Is there anyone else you might know who could help us search?"

Footsteps padded behind us. I turned. Ann. She slipped an arm around me without speaking, and I leaned into her shoulder. Having her close spilled comfort into my veins.

Gabe nodded. "I'll ask Cat to do what he can, too. He has contacts. And..." He paused and looked at me. "Clara could help."

I shut my eyes. "Gabe..."

"She knows a lot of people in the city," he said. "She's a logical choice to help us."

"No." I wasn't desperate enough to involve a potential traitor, someone who'd already betrayed me once, someone I couldn't trust for a moment.

"Let's focus on the plan, shall we?" Adam said.

"I'll speak with Cat tomorrow." Gabe rubbed his forehead and avoided my eyes. "He has contacts all through the workers section."

"And Korr?" I asked.

"I'll deal with him," Ann said.

~

Gabe and I slipped through the streets of Astralux together. We didn't speak as we moved through the throngs of people crowding the sidewalks. The mist curled around us, dampening our hair and coats and making our faces moist. Steamcoaches and carriages rumbled past in the streets, splashing muddy water over our feet.

My chest hummed with anxiety. Every minute that we didn't find Borde was another minute of Jonn's life that slipped away like the mist through my fingers, another minute that the capsule in Ivy's body continued to dissolve.

Gabe caught my eye and smiled faintly to show that he understood. He reached out for my hand, and I let him take it. He gave my fingers a squeeze, and I drew a shuddering breath.

"We'll find him," he said just before we turned the corner that led to Ferris's door. "Clara knows some people who can ask around."

"I told you I don't want her involved in this," I said. "Gabe, you suspect her of being a spy. You think she might have betrayed your family."

Gabe blanched. I stopped and grabbed his arm.

"You already told her, didn't you?"

He bit his lip. His eyelids fluttered as he squinted toward the street. "Lia—"

"No," I said, my voice low and sharp. "I told you no. And you did it anyway."

"She knows the city well. She has many contacts, more than anyone else on our team. She can help us."

"Do not involve me in your misguided attempts to validate her usefulness. I do not trust her, she might be a spy, and now you could have put my family's lives in further danger!"

"Or I could have saved them," Gabe hissed.

I shook my head. Fury made it hard to see straight. Whirling, I stalked for Ferris's door and slammed my fist against it.

The knob turned, and Ferris appeared. He listened for a moment to the sound of my ragged breathing, then Gabe's quiet footsteps as he approached.

"Gabe," he guessed. "And your friend. Lia? Has she been running? She sounds winded."

I didn't speak. I couldn't form words. I cast a wrathful glance at Gabe, and he cleared his throat.

"We wanted to know if you had found any information."

Ferris leaned against the doorframe.

"It's been a tricky business finding this man. He's a slippery one. Doesn't leave much of a trail. But I did find one thing."

"Yes?" Gabe said, hope blossoming in his voice.

"A man calling himself Falcon has been making inquiries about this person."

He handed Gabe a scrap of paper, and I drew closer to see what was written on it. A single word.

Alice.

"Alice?" I asked. "Alice who? Was there any other name, any other identifying information?"

Ferris shrugged. "No. I don't know who she is, or what it means, but I can keep looking."

"Yes, please do," Gabe said, and slipped him a handful of coins.

Ferris closed the door, and we returned to the street. Gabe stole nervous glances at me, but my anger at him had been temporarily waylaid with this recent development. *Alice.* The name hummed in my mind as I turned it over and over. Who was Alice? Why was Borde looking for her? Did she have the device?

"We'll tell Cat and Adam, and they can use this new information to search," Gabe said. He didn't mention Clara.

I was too deep in thought to respond.

~

Aaron's face revealed nothing as I sat across from him in the library. We were alone. I'd hoped perhaps if we spoke one on one, I might have a better chance of convincing him to talk. I was familiar looking at least. Maybe that meant something to him. He clearly didn't trust any of us, but especially not the others.

It was a slim hope, but hope nonetheless.

He looked much better now—color had returned to his face with the regular meals and bathing, and his hair was clean and slightly curly. When he gave me a belligerent look, he reminded me of Ivy, and it made my chest ache with a mixture of bewildering and painful emotions.

I cleared my throat and arranged my features into a neutral expression. "We've been making inquiries in the city. We've learned some new information. Information about Borde's mission here."

Aaron didn't say anything.

"Who is Alice?" I asked.

His eyes widened slightly before narrowing into slits. "I don't know."

"You're lying. Borde is looking for her. Who is she? A friend? A descendant? What's her family name? Does she know about the device?"

He shook his head.

I leaned forward. Frustration welled inside me, forcing itself out the corners of my eyes in furious moisture. Tears.

Aaron studied me, a mixture of suspicion and concern lining his features.

"You never cried as a child," he said, his tone softening.

The quiet observation—and the past it recalled—made me flinch. "I don't cry now," I snapped, ignoring the moisture in my eyes that belied my words. "Now tell me."

"I can't. It's not my story to tell."

I took a deep breath. Everything inside me screamed to shake him, to slap him, to do anything to get him to talk.

He wasn't responding to our threats.

"Jonn looks like you," I said. Every word hurt to speak, but I kept saying them. I kept pushing forward. "He has your eyes, your mouth. Your hair."

"So you said before," he said, and hesitated. "You look like your mother."

I touched my face. "Ivy looks the most like her."

His eyes were dark, full of wonder. "Ivy," he said, as if tasting the name on his tongue. "What is she like?"

"She's stubborn and fierce and brave. She's strong. She befriended the Watchers."

His eyebrows shot to his hairline. "Befriended the *Watchers?*"

"Much has happened since you've been gone."

"It seems so."

I waited.

"I'm sorry," he said, his voice hoarse. "I'm sorry for what you've endured. I'm sorry I was gone. I can't change the past, but I can help you now."

"I know you don't trust me and my friends," I said. "And I respect that. But maybe we can still help each other."

He nodded.

"Tell me about Alice. Who is she?"

Aaron sighed. "Alice isn't a *she*. Alice isn't a person at all."

I stared at him. "What do you mean, Alice isn't a person?"

Aaron's shoulders rose and fell as he took a deep breath. "It's the device."

EIGHTEEN

"I WANT TO know why the Dictator wanted Falcon arrested," Adam said as we spoke later in the conservatory. He sat on a bench, his chin resting in his hand and his eyes following me as I paced up and down the path. "Did he know Falcon is really Meridus Borde, time traveler from the Frost's past, or had he simply gotten into some trouble since his arrival?"

I stopped and considered the question. "They couldn't have known exactly who they were searching for, at any rate, not if they accidentally arrested Aaron in his place," I said after a moment. "They're nothing alike in appearance or age."

Adam nodded. "True."

I resumed pacing. We were at another dead end. We didn't know what Alice was, so it was no help in finding Borde, and we were running out of time. Anxiety gnawed a hole in my stomach.

"This Alice device Borde is looking for," Adam said after a pause. "Aaron knows nothing about what it's for?"

"He said he didn't, and I think he's being truthful."

Adam's brow furrowed. "If we knew what it was, we might have a chance of determining who else might know about it, or where it might be."

"I think there's little chance of that."

Stymied, I sank down on the bench beside him. We sat together like that, our shoulders centimeters apart, not touching but close enough to feel the heat between us. A slow, hot energy began to build along my skin, raising the hairs on my arms and making my insides prickle and twist. I turned my head and found him watching me. Our eyes held. An invisible cord between us tightened.

Footsteps crunched on the path behind us, and the spell was broken. The air cleared and sound rushed in—the drip of rain against the glass, the echo of servants' voices somewhere far away. A regretful smile touched Adam's mouth. It vanished as he turned and stood to meet the person who had intruded on our solitude.

It was Korr. His stopped on the path a few feet from the bench. His gaze flicked between us, and he smirked briefly before his eyes hardened again. "Your ability to toy with two men at once is admirable, if rather tragic for the men."

"What do you want?" I demanded, stung by his words.

He crossed his arms. "You promised me a man who could make the gate work for me."

He was not going to accept another excuse about Aaron needing time to rest. I knew I needed to tell him something. Anything.

I took a deep breath as I looked at Korr. His mouth was curving into a scowl as he saw the hesitation on my face, and I knew he was thinking I'd lied to him, and he was thinking of how he would punish us all for that mistake. His gloved hands twitched, and his shoulders straightened into a line as sharp as a knife blade.

Desperation and anger swirled through my veins. I had to think. I stared at the ground, at the path lined with stones. Stones.

Stone.

The Wanderers.

"This revolution of yours. You have soldiers?"

Korr turned back to face me. "I have men," he said.

"Enough men?"

He was silent.

"I can get you more manpower for your revolution if you give me more time."

Korr licked his lower lip. "What kind of manpower?"

"Lots of it. Hungry for vengeance, too." I remembered the stories I'd heard about how the Wanderers had been driven north.

"How much time do you need?"

"Three days," I said. My heart thudded. He would refuse, surely.

Korr held my gaze for the space of six heartbeats. "Three days."

I didn't exhale until he'd turned on his heel and left the conservatory, and then I sagged and put a hand over my eyes.

"An interesting choice, making more promises that you aren't sure you can keep," Adam commented.

"What else could I do? He was ready to throw me out, or worse. I have no doubt that man is capable of killing those he no longer trusts, and I need shelter and resources if I want to find Borde."

Adam didn't disagree. His eyes softened as he looked at me, and he looked apprehensive, but all he said was, "Take care. You've got a lot of things in the air, and you're juggling with knives now."

~

That afternoon, Gabe joined me as I once again faced Aaron in an attempt to wring clues from him about Borde's location.

"Why is the Alice device in Astralux?" I asked. "Did Borde say anything that might give you any idea as to what it could be, or where?"

Aaron shook his head. "No. Nothing."

"What did he say about it exactly?" Gabe pressed.

"Not much. He said it was a device that he needed to find. He said it had been lost to him in his time, but he could recover it here. He knew who had it. That was what he believed anyway."

"Lost to him in his time," I repeated. "Stolen?" I thought of Gordon and what he'd attempted to do with the PLD.

Aaron considered this suggestion. "Perhaps. He seemed angry whenever he spoke about it, as if it were missing due to a great wrong."

"You say he knew who had it? Is it with a person?"

"No," Aaron said. "I don't think so He was searching old records, going out at odd times. Buying shovels. I think wherever it is, he expected to have to excavate."

Excavate. I chewed my lip. "So someone stole it and buried it, perhaps? And for some reason Borde can't get to it in his time, but he believes he'll be able to find it here. Why this time? Why not any other time?"

Aaron lowered his head. "He believed perhaps he could reunite me with my family. He liked that idea. I hadn't told him that...that I might not want to."

I pushed away the spark of pain that shot through me at his words. I needed to focus on finding the device, and Borde with it. "Do you remember anything else, anything at all?"

Aaron shook his head.

"So if someone stole the Alice device, he must have run with it," I mused. "Taken it far away from the Frost. But why here?"

Gabe stared at a point on the wall, thinking. "There have always been legends of Ancient Ones living on this plain once. Perhaps he believes there are ruins here, beneath the city."

"Can you find out if there are?"

"I'll ask my contacts." Gabe rose and headed for the door. He paused with one hand on the knob. "We'll find it, Lia."

I hoped he was right.

~

Adam, Ann, and I spent the hours after dinner pouring over books about the past. They were mostly worthless— collections of fantastic legends that told us nothing of value. Gabe was still gone, speaking to Ferris and Cat and perhaps others about what they might know or be able to find out.

Ann perched on the window seat, books filling her lap and spilling onto the cushions around her. She chewed her lip absently as she read. Adam occupied the writing desk, methodically flipping through pages and making notes on a piece of paper. I was on my feet, pacing as I read, worrying and sweating at the fact that we were so close and still so far.

"Here's something," Ann said, and we both went still to listen.

She held aloft a book entitled *The Glorious History of Astralux and the Surrounding Territories.* "It says, 'Regarding the origins of the Bakers' District, legend says that it once was the location of a camp of Ancients that was destroyed in a great battle. The foundations of some of the ancient structures are said to still exist beneath the streets today.'"

"The Bakers' District," I repeated. "I passed through there after arriving in Astralux. It's large, crowded. If something is buried there, how on earth are we supposed to even find it, let alone dig it up?"

"There's more," Ann said. "According to this book, 'Some believe an old set of tunnels beneath the city, now used for carrying waste to the river, once belonged to this camp of the Ancients.'"

"We've got to find those tunnels," I said. "When can we go?"

"Night will be best," Adam mused. "We need to assemble what we'll need. Shovels, pickaxes, lanterns. We'll need enough people to help us dig, and we don't exactly know what we're looking for, not yet. These tunnels could span miles. Ann, is there anything else in that book?"

"Nothing," she said, flipping through the pages.

"Maybe Gabe will know something," I said.

A knock sounded at the door. When I opened it, Clara stood outside. We regarded one another for a few seconds before she spoke. "I understand you're looking for someone."

It took all my self-control not to slam the door in her face without replying. "My activities are a private matter." I turned back to the library.

"I have information that might help you."

I stopped.

"Gabe said you were looking for a man who calls himself Falcon," she said.

"Gabe was not supposed to involve you."

She ignored that. "It's an unusual name, Falcon," she said, and paused. "It tends to stick in people's minds. I might have discovered something you'll find interesting."

"Tell me."

"There's been talk of a man asking questions at the Blue Mouse," she said. "It's an inn and tavern. He gives no name, but he told one man that he could leave him an envelope beneath the rain barrels in the square, marked with a sketch of a falcon."

"Where is this inn?" I demanded.

"By Grayman Square, in the Bakers' District."

My heart stuttered at *Bakers' District*. I shut the door and leaned against it to steady myself as I absorbed the news, and the realization that I might have just found the clue that would find Borde and this mysterious device.

"What is it?" Adam asked, his tone half wary, half hopeful.

I met his eyes. "I think we've found a place to start looking."

NINETEEN

MIST FILLED GRAYMAN'S Square and made ghostly shapes out of the buildings surrounding it. Lights glowed in some of the windows, casting a streak of gold across the puddles in the street. Somewhere close by, I heard the rattle of a carriage and the mutter of voices, and my stomach twisted. So far, we'd seen no soldiers, nothing to threaten us. Yet we were all wary. An aura of foreboding filled the wet night air and coated my lungs, making it difficult to breathe.

Adam kept pace beside me, silent and grim in his gray coat. A hat hung low over his face, hiding his eyes, and he looked like an Aeralian gentleman out for a stroll, but his movements were too controlled, too careful, too tense for him to be out on a casual walk. Gabe and Cat kept step behind us, speaking in low tones. They too wore gray coats and hats that covered most of their faces, and Gabe also wore an ascot that practically buried his chin to disguise his features further. As they spoke, Gabe laughed quietly under his breath, and the sound of it was foreign to my ears. I almost never heard him laugh. I was glad for his friendship with Cat, glad that something made him happy in this grim time.

The sign for the Blue Mouse appeared out of the mist. We stopped.

Adam glanced at the door. "I'll go inside and see what I can find out."

"I'll scout around and see if there's any sign of those tunnels," Cat volunteered.

"I'll stay with Gabe," I said. "We'll wait for you."

Adam opened the door and stepped into a swath of light and sound. The heavy oak swung shut behind him, plunging us into misty darkness once more as Cat slunk around the side of the building, leaving Gabe and me alone.

Dripping punctuated the silence as unspoken words crawled in my throat.

"Clara told me she talked to you," Gabe said.

"Yes." The word was sharp. "You shouldn't have talked to her. Promise me you didn't tell her anything else."

He was silent.

"Gabe?"

"I...I told her about the device, too," he admitted.

"You did *what?*"

"She's helped us," he protested. "The information she provided has gotten us this far, hasn't it? I thought maybe—"

I didn't wait for him to finish. Words failed me. I clenched my fingers into fists and strode for the door.

"Where are you going?" Gabe called.

I wrenched the door open and stepped inside the inn.

The interior of the Blue Mouse was dark, and smelled of beer and bread. A fire blazed in a cavernous stove at the far end of the room. Stools lined tables shoved against the outer walls. In the center of the room, a man plucked at a stringed instrument and sang in a wailing voice.

I scanned the room for Adam and spotted him leaning against one of the tables, engaged in conversation with a dark-haired woman nursing a pint. They both looked my way as I approached.

"Is everything all right?" Adam asked, subtly shifting his weight toward the door as if he expected a threat to surge inside any moment.

I lifted one shoulder. "Everything is fine." My voice was strained.

Adam smiled at the woman. "Thank you for your help." He straightened and took my arm, pulling me with him toward an empty table. He sank onto a stool and nudged the one across from him with his foot. I sat.

"What?" he asked.

I shook my head. "Gabe..." I stopped. I was reluctant to confide in Adam about this, given the current emotional complexities between us, but the words begged to be spoken. A turmoil of emotion swirled inside me, driving me mad.

Adam studied me but didn't speak. He didn't give me any indication that he wanted to hear more or that he didn't.

I sighed, giving in to the desire to tell him about it against my better judgment. "Gabe continues to confide in Claire, and I don't like it."

"You don't trust her?"

"Of course I don't. Gabe barely trusts her. I think he's trying to prove something to himself, and he's toying with Ivy and Jonn's lives in the process."

Adam said nothing.

I knew what he was thinking. "I'm not jealous. It isn't that."

"Still," he said. "There are unspoken things between you and Gabe, are there not?"

As there are between you and me, I thought, and changed the subject. "What about you? Discover anything?"

"A man had been asking around, but he hasn't been seen in several days. That could mean he's moved on because he's had no luck here, or—"

"Or it could mean he's found the device." Fear spiked in me. Had we come this far only to lose him again?

"Or," Adam said calmly, "it could mean he's in the process of extracting it now."

"Either way, we need to hurry."

Cat was waiting outside when we exited the inn.

"I found something," he reported, excitement leaking into his words. "Down the street, there's a flight of stairs that leads to a drain. It's quite large, and a ladder drops down inside. It might lead to the tunnels you're seeking."

We followed him without a word. Gabe and I avoided each other's gazes, but I hardly thought about that. My body was on fire with hope and fear and anxiety. Was this it?

We reached the steps Cat had spoken of. Rainwater roared below us, spilling into the drain. The top of the ladder poked out of one side of the hole, slick with algae and covered in rust.

"Down there?" Gabe asked over the sound of the water. His face wrinkled with skepticism.

"I'll go," I said.

"I'll go with you," Adam said.

Spray splattered my face as I descended the steps, taking care not to slip on the wet stones. Adam followed me, so close that I could feel the heat of him on my back. We reached the bottom of the stairs and stopped. Slick, algae-coated stone formed a canyon that ended in the drain. The hole guzzled the rainwater like a hungry maw, and the stench of sewage filled the air.

Adam lifted the lantern and peered down the hole. He motioned for me to follow. The lantern winked in his hand like a star.

"Will it be extinguished in the mist?" I shouted over the roar.

He considered this, probing the places where the glass met the iron, then he removed his cloak and wrapped it around the lantern. Gabe and Cat stirred above us, silent as they peered down into the sudden darkness.

Adam grabbed the edge of the ladder with one hand and began to descend. His knuckles whitened around the cuff of stone that rimmed the top of the drain, and his body and then his head were swallowed by the darkness. Another moment and he was gone completely.

I looked at Gabe and Cat for reassurance, but they had vanished. My blood sang a song of fear in my veins as I drew in a lungful of the putrid air and stuck my foot in the blackness of the drain.

My foot found the first rung of the ladder, and I lowered myself onto it. Cool air swirled around my legs, the spray of the water soaking my coat and the tendrils of my hair that had escaped from my bun. I took another step down, and another. The circle of black sky above me began to shrink, and with each step I took, my stomach squeezed tighter. I took deep breaths and kept moving. I'd faced more frightening things before, but I hated the dark. Anything could attack, and I'd have no way to know what I was fighting. My skin prickled in anticipation of steel sinking into my skin with every step down the ladder.

My feet finally touched stone, and I relinquished my hold on the metal rung above me. A chaotic darkness swirled around me, made of mist and a roaring cacophony of falling water.

"Adam?" My whisper mingled with the sound of the water and was swept away.

Light flooded the tunnel as Adam released the lantern from the cage of his coat. Fog clouded the glass. Droplets of water glimmered on his cheeks and chin, and his hair clung to his forehead. His chest rose and fell as he met my eyes. I looked past him, examining the area. Walls of thick stone surrounded us above and on either side. A narrow ledge ran alongside the water, disappearing in the darkness in either direction.

"Which way do we go?"

"Pick a direction," he answered. "Your guess is as accurate as mine."

I chose left.

We had to step along the ledge one at a time. The sound of falling water faded as we went deeper and deeper into the tunnel, replaced by sounds of dripping and suspicious splashes in the water below us. Something skittered across my feet, and I bit my lip to hold back a startled cry. The lantern dipped and flickered, and our shadows danced in its light.

Faintly, another light appeared ahead. I grabbed Adam's arm. He nodded; he'd seen it, too. We advanced slowly. The ledge widened into a path of stone. The ceiling closed in as we turned a corner, almost low enough to touch.

A torch lay on the ground ahead of us, burning brightly. Signs of excavation surrounded it—piles of dirt, displaced stones, a shovel. My heart stuttered and my breath caught. Borde?

That was when I heard the sound of footsteps echoing through the tunnel.

Too many footsteps to be one man.

Adam pulled me back. "Soldiers," he hissed.

We ran. Shouts echoed behind us, and I didn't look back until we'd reached the ladder. Light filled the tunnels, and shadows leaped against the walls. The scrape and clatter of stones filled the air, punctuated by the bark of commands. The voices rang with triumph.

They were taking it. Whatever it had been, they were taking it. My eyes burned, although they were dry of tears. I forced myself to climb the ladder back to the surface, and Adam was right behind me. The spray from the water pouring down the drain drenched my face and coat, but I didn't pause. I reached the top and inhaled the scent of damp sewage and fresh air.

"Lia!" Gabe's low cry caught my attention. He and Cat appeared out of the darkness as Adam and I struggled out of the hole. "Did you—?" He stopped, scanning my empty hands. "You didn't find it?"

"Worse," I said. "Soldiers got there first."

"Soldiers?" Cat repeated. "In the tunnels?"

"Yes." I held Gabe's gaze. Heat simmered in my chest, a fury building and threatening to choke me. "Soldiers."

We retreated to the shadow of a shop. Silver light glittered on wet cobblestones and shone on the water pouring into the tunnel.

"I should go back," Adam said softly. "Maybe Borde returned to the site to see if the soldiers took the device. He might be there now."

It was a far-fetched hope, but I nodded, barely conscious of his words over the roaring in my ears. Dimly, I heard Cat say something about scouting the street for any sign of them. I was still staring at Gabe. When they'd both left us, the words hit my tongue, and they tasty bitter.

"You know who did this."

Gabe flinched. "We can't be sure—"

"Gabe," I snapped. "You cannot continue to endanger us all by harboring her, not if she's betraying us."

He turned away, his body sharp edges of anger and denial where the moonlight touched the line of his shoulders, the cut of his cheekbones, the slash of his mouth. "Will you tell anyone?" His voice was just a rasp in the silence.

The raw agony in his tone deflated me a little. "Not if you tell her to leave."

"I...I will. I promise."

"Do it, and do it immediately."

Footsteps rang on the street behind us. We both straightened, dropping the topic as Cat joined us. "No sign of them," he said. "Where's Adam?"

"He hasn't returned yet."

Cat's gaze darted between us. "What's wrong?"

"Nothing," Gabe said.

"I don't want to discuss it," I said at the same time.

Cat's eyebrows lifted, but he wisely left the matter alone.

A clink met my ears. Adam's head emerged from the drain. He hauled himself up and wiped his forehead with his wrist. I went to meet him, and the defeat in his eyes shook me to my core.

"Well?" I whispered, still daring to hope.

"If it was there," he said, "they took it. I didn't find Borde."

The hope in my chest shattered, slicing my insides like broken glass, but I wasn't ready to quit yet.

"We should make one sweep of the area before we leave," I said. "If Borde fled, he probably didn't go far. He must be as frantic as we are to recover this device."

Gabe looked at me. I avoided his eyes. "You two should go," I said. "Gabe might be recognized come daybreak."

He nodded and joined Cat, and they slipped up the street and out of sight.

Adam observed me without comment, and I silently thanked him for being the type who valued silence over pestering questions. The issue with Gabe was too raw to revisit. I needed time to process my anger at what had happened, but I couldn't contemplate that now. We needed to look for Borde; perhaps we could still find him.

We checked the alleys and corners, looking in any place that someone might seek refuge during the wee hours between dawn and day. A few ragged beggars peered at us, curiosity plain in their eyes, but there was no sign of the white-haired scientist we sought. The horizon turned pale with the coming morning, and a light rain began to fall. The hiss of it surrounded us in a gray cocoon, sealing us inside our own bubble of sorrow.

Adam turned a restless circle in the street. "He must have decided to put distance between himself and the soldiers rather than stay to observe."

Exhaustion pulled at my limbs. I wanted to sink down onto the street and go to sleep, but we couldn't stop looking.

"We have to find him. He has to be here."

"Lia—"

"No," I snapped. "We can't give up."

Adam touched my arm. "I know," he said. "But we're both spent. Let's get something to eat and rest for a short while. After, we can continue."

I let him lead me toward a bakery. I recognized it. I'd gotten directions to the Plaza of Horses there after I'd informed Adam that I was leaving the Thorns. It felt like a lifetime ago.

The bell above the door jingled as we stepped inside, and the warm scent of baking goods enveloped us. Gaslights burned brightly on the green paneled walls, dispelling the lingering darkness of the rainy morning. The baker was nowhere to be seen.

Adam rang the bell for service while I drifted to the window to stare at the street. Rain pattered gently at the window. A few pedestrians scurried past, their coats pulled snug about their necks and their hats shoved down over their faces.

My panic was beginning to settle like dust along my bones, thickening into a feeling more akin to weary defeat. In my mind's eye, I saw my brother, thin and brittle beneath the quilts, his cheeks porcelain, and his fingers restless as he slept the sleep of the near-dead. I saw Ivy toppling over, succumbing to the Sickness and the coma that set in swiftly after infection. I bit my lip so hard that I tasted blood. My nails dug into my palms.

The door opened and closed, the bell jingled, and I turned reflexively to glance at the newcomer. A pair of bright eyes met mine from beneath the brim of a hat. A wrinkled mouth fell opened in astonishment. All the air sucked from my lungs in one gasp.

Borde.

TWENTY

I COULDN'T SPEAK, couldn't draw breath. The air chilled, sound ceased, and the room darkened as I stared into the eyes of the man I'd been seeking for so long.

He was thinner than I remembered. His hair fell in shaggy waves to his shoulders, and new wrinkles enfolded his eyes and the corners of his mouth. Thick new scars crossed his forehead and cheeks in pale, white lines. He wore a tattered coat and a pair of patched trousers. A timepiece dangled from his vest, the glass cracked.

"Lia Weaver," he said as he looked at me. Astonishment leaked into every syllable. "You never cease to amaze me. How...?"

"It's a long story." I didn't know where to begin. The weight of everything that must be said pressed against me. I sorted my words, choosing them with care. "I've been looking for you. We must talk at once."

Out of the corner of my eye, I saw Adam turn his head to look at us.

Borde darted a glance around the shop. "Not here. It isn't safe."

Adam left the counter and joined me.

"Who is he?" Borde demanded, taking a step back.

"A friend," I said. I reached out one hand and touched his wrist. "Come, I have a safe place where we can talk"—I lowered my voice—"about the device."

Borde licked his lips. "How do you know about that?"

"I'll explain as soon as I can. Please."

I could see the struggle in his eyes. He trusted me, but he was wary all the same. "All right," he said.

We left the bakery and traveled quickly and without speaking through the streets. People began to crowd the sidewalks and alleyways, appearing from the early morning mist like ghosts. Sweat dripped between my shoulder blades as we passed a pair of soldiers on the corner, but their gazes passed over us as if we were invisible.

The worn stones and rusted steel of the city began to give way to wide thoroughfares lined with gas streetlamps. Borde followed us without a word, but his eyes widened as we passed stone walls and coach houses. Finally, the pointed gables and arching windows of Korr's estate appeared from the mist as we rounded the final corner, and I exhaled in relief. Almost there. We slipped inside the yard just as the sun began to rise amid the rainclouds.

"Hurry," I urged, quickening my pace. "We don't want to be seen."

Once inside, we ascended the staircase and went straight to the library. As soon as the door clicked shut, I turned to face the scientist, my mouth full of questions and my heart full of hope.

"Tell me everything," Borde begged. "How do you know about the device? What do you know?"

A startled gasp cut me off, and I turned to see Aaron standing in the shadows of the room, looking dazed.

"I was waiting for you to return," he said to me, his voice trailing off as he stared at Borde. "I must have dozed off... Meridus?"

"Aaron," Borde said, delight filling his voice. They embraced each other with a familiarity and ease that made my chest clench with abrupt and bewildering envy.

"I returned and you were gone—"

"They came for you. They took me instead. I gave my name as Falcon."

I stopped listening to the explanations. I met Adam's eyes over the tops of their heads. He nodded to me, and I dragged in a deep breath.

"Please," I said. "We must talk."

Borde turned to face me, and his expression faded to a somber one as he glimpsed the look on my face.

I explained tersely what Gordon had done to Ivy, and Borde's brow darkened with anger. Absently, he rubbed the scars that crisscrossed his face as he listened without comment until I'd finished.

"I believe he's telling the truth about knowing the cure," Borde said. "Gordon escaped shortly after you left my time, and he began working for another facility. The reports from that place said they had found a breakthrough, but by then, it was too late for it to matter."

"So you know the cure? You'll help me?"

"I do not know the cure for the Sickness," Borde said.

Breathe. I sucked in air, forcing myself to push through the disappointment threatening to swallow me whole. "And now soldiers have taken the device." Despair swirled around me, threatening to drown me. Everything I'd done, I'd done for my family's safety and welfare. Now I would lose them both, despite every effort I'd made, despite traveling to Aeralis, leaving the Thorns, dealing with Korr, breaking into a prison camp, searching and finding Borde...

"What if we fake the device? Create a replica. You know what it looks like. You can help us."

"Gordon will want to see it work before he does anything for you," the scientist said.

A sob stuck in my throat, choking me. I turned toward the window. Adam was beside me in the next moment, his hands finding my shoulders. My eyes burned and my body shook as I let him fold me to him.

A single idea pushed through the sorrow, a solitary nudge against the frozen crust of defeat that was already forming in my thoughts. I raised my head.

"Soldiers took the Alice device. So I assume the device has been taken to the Dictator's palace?" I asked.

Borde and Aaron looked at me, uncomprehending. Adam's hands stilled on my back.

"Borde?" I asked.

"Yes," he said. "It would have been taken there. He has scientists who would study it."

"You need the device so badly you'd travel through time to retrieve it. I need Gordon to think I'm giving it to him so he'll heal my brother and sister. Surely we can come to an agreement of mutual assistance."

Borde stared at me, his mouth slightly open. "Go on."

"What if we could somehow get the device back from the palace? Korr is plotting a revolution, after all. That should count for something."

Borde shook his head. "As soon as word of a coup reaches the ears of those who guard such a device, I fear they will destroy it."

"Not if we can get it before they know what's happening."

~

I headed for the library, where I would meet Adam and Borde to discuss our plans for linking the gate and the PLD. The timing would be delicate, as both would need to be activated in order for a successful jump to take place.

The faint, harsh murmur of voices made me pause outside the conservatory. Gabe's voice. He sounded troubled.

"I didn't do it," a female voice insisted.

Clara.

Gabe's reply was too low to hear.

I crept closer to the door and hesitated. I didn't want to eavesdrop, but I needed to be sure he was doing what he'd promised. She'd sold us out to the Dictator, and because of her, Jonn and Ivy's lives still hung in the balance. If he wouldn't deal with her, I would.

Footsteps rang out, and Clara slipped through the door. She almost collided with me as she rushed past without a word. Gabe appeared a moment after. His shoulders slumped as he caught sight of me. "You heard?"

I didn't reply. I looked at him, the question apparent on my face.

"I did as you asked," he growled, and started past me.

"Don't," I snapped, grabbing his sleeve. "Don't play the martyr with me. My siblings might die because of what she did. Be glad she's walking away from this."

He pulled his arm away and stalked down the hall.

Anger simmered in my veins. I headed for the library. Inside, Adam, Borde, Ann, and Aaron waited for me.

"The gate and the portable locomotion device must both be open simultaneously for a jump to be successful," Borde explained after we'd all gathered. "However, the PLD is not able to remain active indefinitely, at least not by its own power. But there might be a way for me to temporarily work around this problem. According to Gabe, Korr is already in possession of a device I invented that will let us connect the PLD to another power source. He received it from a spy who found it in the Echlos ruins."

"Who stole it from a Thorns operative," Adam corrected with a frown.

I shot a glance at him. Why hadn't I heard about this?

"Nevertheless, we have it now," Borde said. "I must examine it further, but I think it can be done. After that, I'll journey to Echlos and activate the gate there. As it's still connected to its power source, it should be able to run almost indefinitely..." He broke off, muttering to himself and scribbling in the air with his fingers, as if etching plans on a giant, invisible chalkboard.

"I'll return with Borde to Iceliss once you've got it sorted out," I said.

"I want to come with you, too," Ann said.

Adam nodded at me to show that he too would accompany us.

We looked at Aaron. He looked at Borde as if for help.

"I need him to remain here," Borde said. "To manage the PLD. Besides, Korr still thinks he's Falcon."

"Yes," Aaron agreed hastily. "That might be best."

He didn't want to face Jonn and Ivy. A dull resentment burned briefly in my chest, but I shoved it away. There was no time for those feelings now.

"Let me know when you're ready to leave," I said.

~

The wind whipped tendrils from my braid and made them dance around my face. The horse beneath me snorted and strained at the bit, wanting to run with the scent of the earth and grass that teased his nostrils. Adam rose beside me, and as Astralux disappeared into the mist behind us, he pulled a pale blue cloak from his pack and wrapped it about his shoulders before handing another to me.

The faintest scent of ice rode on the wind, and I tasted the promise of bone-shattering cold. Excitement hummed in my veins.

We were returning to the Frost.

TWENTY-ONE

SNOW FELL FROM the sky, swirling around my cheeks and sticking to the edges of my cloak. The path before us glimmered with melting ice and the storm-blown petals of the snow blossoms that lined the edges of the forest. The colors swirled and melted together as the wind made the flowers and branches of the trees dance amid the fall of fresh snow. Everything was gray and white and green and blue.

"A spring snow," I explained to Borde, who craned his neck to see everything above and around him. "We're in the Thaw, so it won't stick for long." The words left my lips in a plume of white. Cold bit my ears and fingers, and the feeling was painful pleasure.

I was home.

But something had changed. The wilderness around me retained its wild, stark beauty, but the edge of gritty doom had been removed, bathed instead with the comfort of safety. The light bathing the woods glowed. The once-desperate hiss of the wind over the icy rocks now sounded like soft chimes. Instead of claws of fear digging into my stomach, I felt peace.

Everything had changed since we'd driven out the Aeralian soldiers, since we'd unlocked the secrets of the Watchers, since we'd made it safe for our people to travel the Frost. I just hadn't felt it until I'd left and returned.

"I recognize this place!" Borde shouted as we reached the hill that looked over Iceliss. He turned to me with an expression of utter astonishment, and I tried to see the village below from his eyes. The weathered stone, cracked and stained from centuries of exposure to the harsh elements, stood amid the steel remnants of the Farther occupation. Snow blossoms bloomed in a protective ring around the town and adorned the Cages leading to the gate. In the streets, men and women clad in cloaks of blue, gray, and white scurried between the houses. Snow trickled from the sky and painted everything a soft, pale color as curls of smoke reached up from the houses, gray mingling with gray.

We dismounted at the gate. People murmured and whispered as they caught sight of us. No one said anything, but a few eyes narrowed at the sight of the former Mayor's daughter.

Borde returned the villagers' stares with frank curiosity. "Incredible," he murmured. "Just look at them."

Adam caught my arm. "Time is limited," he whispered into my ear. "I can accompany Borde to Echlos. You should find Ivy, see Jonn."

Make sure he was still alive, is what he didn't say. I nodded. My blood was chilly as river water.

"Do you need me to go with you?" Ann asked, laying a hand on my wrist.

"I want to go alone, I think," I told her. "Go with Adam and Borde." I looked at Adam. "We can discuss what needs to be done after he's seen the gate."

Adam nodded. After a moment's hesitation, he reached out and touched my cheek. The brush of his fingers gave me strength.

I watched them ride away, and then I turned in the direction of the house at the highest point in the village, the Mayor's house.

I needed to see to my brother and sister.

~

The Healer at Jonn's door lifted his head in surprise at the sight of me. "Bluewing," he said. "You've returned."

"Have you seen my sister?"

"She's in the Frost with the Watchers," he said. "She'll return before night."

Irritation flared in me, mingled with fear. How could she continue to wander the Frost alone after what had happened? I took a deep breath. The worst had already happened. I might as well be calm about it.

The Healer studied me, taking in the Frost cloak thrown over my Aeralian garments. His eyebrows lifted, but he didn't comment. When his eyes returned to mine, I saw the trust in them, despite my new Farther appearance.

I looked at the door, my mouth dry. "Jonn?"

The Healer hesitated, and my stomach fell like a stone.

"Lingering," he said.

I exhaled. Still alive. Still here. Tears threatened to blur my vision, and I blinked hard. My fingers were clumsy as I fumbled with my cloak, removing it. The hall was too stifling, too hot.

"May I see him?"

The Healer nodded and stepped aside, and I went in.

Stillness wrapped the room in a suffocating blanket. Jonn lay on the bed, his skin the color of ash, his hands like claws on the quilt. Dark hollows made his face look like a skull. His eyes were closed, and his lids trembled as I approached, but he didn't open them. His mouth twitched as if he were dreaming.

I sank down beside him. It seemed impossible to speak above a whisper. The air felt sacred.

"Jonn?"

His eyelids twitched again as if he'd heard me. Veins bulged across the delicate skin and snaked across his cheeks. His chest rose and fell in shallow breaths.

The anxiety that had long lived in my chest just below my heart began to turn to sheer pain. "Stay," I panted. "Please stay. Don't die. Don't leave me. I've done so much, Jonn. Please."

Silence.

I couldn't say anything else, so I just sat there, one hand on the quilt inches from his, strangling in my grief.

But Jonn never woke.

Minutes or hours passed. I couldn't be sure in the gloom of the sickroom silence. I measured time by the number of breaths my brother dragged through his inflamed nostrils, by the number of times his fingers shivered against the blankets. Finally, I rose and went to the door. I had to find my sister. I had to speak to the others. I had to rest.

The Healer stood as I exited.

"He didn't wake," I reported dully.

"He never does anymore. It is expected." The Healer paused. "If there is no intervention found for him, he will not last more than another week or two."

My chest squeezed. I nodded and left.

The period of contagiousness was long past, so I did not have to burn my clothes. Still, I washed and rewashed my hands in the basin in the room I'd shared with Ivy. Exhaustion made my eyes feel rusty. My bones ached with every movement I made. Going to the bed, I sank onto it and looked at the plaster ceiling.

The door opened, and Ivy rushed in.

"Lia!"

She collided with me in a smack of wind-chapped flesh and a swirl of snow-soaked cloak. I held her back by her shoulders to look at her, and although she seemed thinner and paler than before, she was unchanged in her energy levels.

"How do you feel?"

"I feel just like my old self," Ivy said, waving a hand dismissively. "They told me you'd returned with Adam and Ann. And a stranger." Hope blazed on her face. "Who—?"

"Borde, the scientist. He's going to fix the gate and we're going to get that device." I hesitated, biting my lip. "But there are still many things to be done before you can be well."

"Things?"

"Never mind that at the moment. Tell me more about your health."

Ivy wiggled away, her face wrinkling in a scowl. "I'm perfectly fine. Everyone is fussing over me."

"Everyone?"

She hesitated. "The Healers say I look ill. They've been trying to keep me indoors."

"Why do they say you're ill?"

She didn't seem to want to answer that. "I've been fine," she said.

"And the raccoon? How is he faring?"

At that question, her face fell, and she bit her lip and didn't respond.

"Ivy. You have to rest."

"How long until you go away again?" she asked, ignoring my words.

"Days, perhaps. Or less. There isn't much time."

"There never is," she said sadly.

I hesitated, thinking of Aaron. I needed to tell her. "Ivy...I found...I found our father."

Her forehead wrinkled, and then her eyes widened as she bolted up from the bed. "Our father?"

I winced at that descriptor. "He was in a prison camp outside Astralux. He'd assumed the name Falcon. We rescued him, thinking we were rescuing Borde."

"A prison camp? I don't understand."

I tried to explain as best as I could about the fugitive, Aaron's fall through the gate, and the subsequent need for a replacement. Ivy listened without comment until I'd finished. She took a deep breath.

"Where is he now?"

"Still in Aeralis."

Her eyes shimmered with curiosity. There was no sign of anger or bitterness in her expression. "You're angry," she observed.

"Ivy," I said. "He doesn't want to see us. He doesn't seem to even want to acknowledge us, let alone want to be our father."

"It must be a lot for him to take in," she murmured.

"He left us!"

"Not on purpose. Not according to his story."

"Yes, but..." I searched for words to describe the turmoil I felt about the subject. "When he had the chance to come back, he didn't."

"These things take time, sometimes. People can't just snap their fingers and feel the way they're supposed to," she said.

I sighed. Her words goaded me, but I couldn't deny them. "Where do you get such thoughts, Wise One?"

She shrugged. "It's happened here, hasn't it? We have peace, and yet many of us struggle to leave our homes after dark. Despite the protection most now have against the Watchers, many still flinch and cower at the sight of them. Change is happening, but it comes with the speed of melting ice in early spring. Just a trickle at first."

"Are you saying you think Aaron might change his mind about us?"

Ivy smiled in a noncommittal way. "I'm saying be patient with him. That's all." She paused. "Do you want him to?"

"I don't."

Ivy said nothing, but she looked skeptical.

"Anyway," I continued. "It doesn't matter now. I need to find Adam and discuss our plans going forward. Please rest while I'm gone."

She settled on the bed with a sigh, and I started to leave the room when something caught my eye.

The journal. Borde's journal. I would recognize it anywhere. But it looked newer, less cracked and faded. The leather gleamed as I lifted it.

"Don't touch that," Ivy snapped.

I opened the pages. Scrawl stared up at me, words written over and over.

What woven secret will keep you warm?

Ivy snatched it from my hand.

"Ivy?"

"All right," she said. "I'm forgetting things. My memories are hazy sometimes. The Healers say it could be the Sickness. I've been writing this journal to help me remember."

"This journal...you?"

"What is it?" she stared at me.

I shook my head. "I...nothing."

A shiver ran through me as she rushed to hide the book away.

Somehow, Ivy's journal would pass through the portal and be found by Borde in the past.

I put the journal back under the bed without explaining and left the room, my mind churning with questions and thoughts.

~

Wind whipped my hair and stung my cheeks as I slipped down the path toward the Wanderer camp. Two sentries stepped from the trees to intercept me.

"I'm Lia Weaver," I said. "I need to speak to Stone."

They recognized me and nodded. One slipped away as I waited. After a moment, Stone appeared at the edge of the camp.

"Lia Weaver," he said. "You've been gone from the Frost, I hear."

"Yes. Someone threatened my sister. I had to get something to save her life."

He studied me. "And did you obtain this thing?"

"Not quite. Not yet." I took a deep breath. "I have a proposal for you."

~

Adam, Ann, and Borde were waiting for me when I returned. They sat around the grand table in the dining hall, hands clasped and voices only murmurs. I joined them, slipping into a seat as they glanced up at me. I could see the questions in their faces.

"Stone has agreed to join the Restorationist revolution, along with some of the strongest of his people."

Adam nodded without saying anything. Ann sighed in relief.

"But we still have a problem we haven't discussed yet," I said.

Adam lifted one eyebrow, and Ann tipped her head to the side. Borde was muttering to himself, but my words made him pause.

"Borde, you'll be here in Echlos when the palace coup takes place. Adam, you'll have a place there. But what about me? I need to be there. I need to get that device."

"Korr won't want that," Ann said softly. "He won't like that you're changing things on him, not at the last minute."

"We need another promise to offer in order to convince him. Any ideas?"

They were silent.

"I have an idea," a voice said behind us.

I turned. "Ivy, you're supposed to be resting."

She crossed her arms and leaned against the doorframe, ignoring me. "What do we have that Korr doesn't?"

I locked eyes with her, lifting my eyebrows in surprise, and she smiled. "Exactly."

"It would never work."

"It will work, and let me tell you why." She crossed to the table and sat, and we listened as she laid out the plan.

After several hours, eyelids began to droop and heads began to sag forward. We said goodnight, and the others got up to leave.

"Ivy," I said, before she could slip away. "How is the raccoon?"

She paused and chewed her lip. I could tell she didn't want to tell me. That was answer enough, but still, I needed to see.

"Where is it?" I asked.

"He's outside," she said quietly. "Behind the house, in the garden. The Healers wouldn't let me keep him in the house for fear of contamination."

Thank goodness for sensible people. I stood. "Show me?"

She led me through the kitchens and into the garden, where bare patches of mud gleamed in the starlight. The outline of a cage rose from the darkness beneath a tree. Ivy made crooning noises in her throat as she approached it, and then I heard her gasp sharply.

"What? What is it?" I was at her side in two strides.

"Something bit him," Ivy squeaked, putting her fingers against the wire. "Look, his leg."

The raccoon lay on the floor of the cage, its head down in misery. Ivy undid the latch to the door and reached inside. The animal was too sick to try to move away, and she stroked its head gently while singing softly under her breath.

Something fluttered beside her foot. A mothkat. I kicked at it, and the creature took to the sky.

"Poor fellow," Ivy whispered. She looked at me. "I need to tend to this."

"Ivy, it's just going to die."

"Please," she said. "This world is cruel enough. We don't have to be cruel, too."

"There will always be plenty of wounded raccoons, Ivy."

She stared at me stubbornly until I relented, and I stayed with the animal, making reluctant soothing noises, while she went for bandages and salve.

~

Later I found Adam by the fire in the parlor, after night had covered the Frost and wrapped the world in slumber. He sat cross-legged on the carpet, his arms resting on his knees, the firelight playing hide and seek with the shadows on his face. When he heard my footsteps, he stirred and turned to meet me.

"I spoke to the Healer," he said when I didn't speak.

I settled without comment beside him on the ground. "Ivy is in denial, and Jonn grows weaker every day. We are running out of time."

After a moment's hesitation, Adam reached over and drew me into his arms. I put my head on his shoulder and breathed in his scent of earth and pine. I didn't know what this meant, only that I needed it. I shut my eyes and listened to the whisper of the wind at the windowpanes, the crackle of the fire, the beat of Adam's heart.

"The gate?" I asked after a moment.

"Borde needs one more day. Then we must return." He hesitated. "We could look for Gordon."

"No," I said sharply. "If he thinks he's being pursued, he'll infect Ivy."

"If we could somehow make him talk..."

"I hope it doesn't come to that," I said. "Right now I want to find the device, not anger the madman further."

For a moment, silence held us.

Adam shifted. "Do you remember the last time we were here in front of this fire?"

I nodded. It had been the night before he'd left for Aeralis, leaving me behind to manage the Frost alone. Much had changed. Yet here in this place of memory and shadow, so much felt the same.

"Lia," he said. The word rumbled against my cheek as the tenor of his voice changed, roughened. I opened my eyes and drew away, facing him. His eyes were dark and full of secrets.

"This is not the time," he said. "Nor the place, but when you left the Thorns and went out into the streets of Astralux alone, I felt as though a part of me had been ripped away."

A muscle in his jaw twitched, and he turned his head to look at the fire instead of me.

"I'm sorry that I followed you, interfered with your plans. I should have spoken to you directly. It wasn't honorable to your intelligence and strength—to your freedom of choice in the matter—for me to treat you that way, as if you were a subordinate or a child. And I want to treat you honorably. You deserve that from me."

I was still, listening.

Adam turned his head and met my eyes again. Frustration flashed across his face, a rare show of emotion. "I am not the kind who makes long speeches. I don't have any polished poetry to recite for you, not like—" He stopped again and shook his head as if clearing it. "When you are with me, I feel as though I can breathe again after holding my breath for too long. I just want to see you safe and happy, and your family safe and happy...everything and everyone you love safe and happy." He held my gaze. "Everyone," he repeated.

My chest rose and fell as I breathed.

Adam paused. "I just wanted to tell you that I wish you happiness with Gabe, if that's what you desire."

I reached out and took his hand. "Adam."

"No," he said. "Don't try to explain yourself, please. I'm not seeking some kind of declaration from you. Like I said, this is hardly the time or the place. Your family's lives are at stake. We're in the middle of a mission. This isn't the time to make decisions about matters of the heart. I only want you to know where I stand."

"Adam—"

He put a finger to my lips. "Not tonight."

He rose and left me sitting there, filled with confusion. Part of me wanted to run after him and demand that we talk further, but I wasn't the kind to run after people, and Adam wasn't the kind to waste his words.

Every single one he'd spoken to me was precious, and I remembered them as I stared into the fire and listened to the wind until finally, sleep stole over me and lulled me unconscious.

TWENTY-TWO

IT HAD ONLY taken Borde a day to reprogram the gate. A day too short, a day too long. We had no time, and yet my heart throbbed as if bruised at the thought of leaving Jonn and Ivy again.

Adam, Ann, and I met Borde at Echlos in the evening, before the first stars appeared on the horizon. Adam carried a lantern, and Ann's eyes were wide and her lips were pale in the light of it. She'd never made a jump before. I reached out and found her hand as we reached the lowest level of Echlos, where the gate waited. She squeezed my fingers hard without speaking, and we walked the final steps together, connected by warm flesh and hope.

Energy crackled in the air and danced along the hairs of my arms. Sparks sizzled on the snow. I tasted it on my tongue and felt it in my blood. The sleeping eye was awake and open, watching us.

It was time.

There would be no goodbyes. We didn't have the luxury. I'd left Ivy a note explaining that I would be back soon. We'd slipped from the village without fanfare.

"Ready," Borde shouted, scurrying across the expanse of the room toward us. Wind blew through the hole in the ceiling above our heads and whipped his hair back. His scars gleamed in the near-darkness. Behind him, the gate gaped, a maw of glowing energy with a pinprick of blackness in the center.

"I'll go first," Adam said, and handed me the lantern. He stepped toward the darkness and the gate swallowed him whole. I bit my lip as he vanished in the span of a blink.

"I...I should go next," Ann said. Her voice shook faintly.

"It's just a moment of falling," I said. "Don't be afraid."

She released my hand and stepped forward. A rush of wind and burst of energy, and she was gone, too.

A memory tickled my mind. I turned to Borde.

"Before I left your time and returned to mine, you tried to tell me something. What was it?"

Borde sighed. "I was having second thoughts about sending the Sickness back in that box."

I was silent. If only he'd been able to stop me. Would any of this have happened?

"What if we simply used the gate to go back to that moment? What if I could undo it all?"

"We can't change the past," Borde said firmly. "What is done is done."

"Go," I said, when he hesitated longer.

Borde vanished through the portal next, and it was just me. I lifted my eyes to the hole in the roof, where starlight glittered. The glowing red eyes of a Watcher stared down at me. It was drawn to the energy. A growl rumbled in its throat, and snow spilled through the hole as it shifted its claws.

Taking a deep breath, I stepped into the eye of energy, and the wind and cold fire closed around me in a shocking embrace.

~

Darkness swirled around me, and I was falling, falling, falling. I hit the ground with a violent thud and rolled sideways. My vision swam, my head swarmed with pain. A groan forced its way through my lips, and I lay still.

"Lia?"

Gabe's voice hovered somewhere above me. Gentle hands wrapped around my shoulders and helped me up. I struggled to my feet and tried to see, but my head was still spinning. I choked back vomit and leaned against Gabe.

"Where's Ann?" I managed. "Is she all right?"

"She's here," he said. "She's a little sick because she hasn't made several jumps like you."

"This isn't considered sick?" I croaked. My head throbbed as if I'd been kicked by a horse, and nausea made my stomach curl.

A voice laughed near my elbow. "You're doing fine."

Borde.

"I've made dozens of test jumps," he said. "I don't feel the effects anymore. Soon, you won't either."

I cracked open one eye and saw him standing by a swirling circle of light cast by the activated PLD. The glow of it danced on the walls and painted our clothing and hair blue-green. We were in what appeared to be the basement level of Korr's house. Stone walls covered in a web of pipes and whirring mechanical systems surrounded us. The PLD clung like an insect to one of the pipes, bound to it by wire. Another device, smaller and slimmer, connected it with the pipe, and a blinding light glowed in the seams where they touched.

I scanned the rest of the room and spotted Adam, his back to a wall and his head down. Beside him, Ann was curled in a ball of misery, her eyes squeezed shut. Someone knelt beside her and offered her water. Raven. A set of spiral steps led upward to a door, where light poured down in a swath of blinding white.

As I looked, a figure in black stepped into the doorway at the top of the stairs. Korr. He surveyed us, then the PLD. His mouth curled in satisfaction at the sight of us.

"I see you were successful," he said. "It tempers the fact that you decided not to share the truth about who the real Falcon is." He glared at me, then at Borde.

Aaron must have talked, or perhaps Korr was even cleverer than I had considered. It didn't matter now, though.

I met Korr's eyes despite the pain hammering in my skull. "When do we talk plans for the revolution?"

A faint smile touched his lips. "I must say, I'm impressed by your gall. Not surprised, but impressed."

"Well? The plans?"

"As soon as you're able to walk," he said, and left the room in a swirl of his cloak.

~

After the effects of the jump wore off, we met in the dining hall. Korr looked at Borde with undisguised suspicion as soon as the scientist entered the room at my side. "This is a tactical meeting," he said. "What's he doing here?"

"We need him in order to carry out the plan to overthrow the Dictator."

Korr turned his head and pinned me with a glare. "We?"

Fear of his refusal caressed cold fingers down my spine, but I pressed on. "I need something that the Dictator took from Falcon," I explained. "It's in the palace. I have to retrieve it before the coup takes place."

"So let me make sure I have this correct," Korr said. "You talked me into helping you rescue Falcon in exchange for his services to me, but it turns out he wasn't Falcon after all, a fact that you hid from me after you discovered it, and now that you've found the real Falcon, you need something else from me?"

"Oh," I said. "I'm prepared to offer something you're going to want very, very much."

Korr raised one eyebrow an infinitesimal amount. His lips twisted in a disbelieving scowl, but I had his attention. "Oh?"

I leaned forward and steepled my fingers, mimicking one of his favorite gestures. "Let me tell you how."

He listened as I laid out the plan Ivy had crafted. My heart thumped against my ribs, but I kept a tight smile on my lips. I couldn't let him see how frightened I was of the possibility that he'd refuse. My expression was hammered steel, but beneath the table, my legs felt as gooey as unbaked bread. When I'd finished, I sat back and crossed my arms.

Korr took his time responding. Finally, he shifted in his chair and said, "You must do exactly as I say if I am to say yes."

"Did I mention I procured those extra soldiers for you, too?"

He sighed.

I exhaled quietly. "You won't be disappointed. We all want the same things, Korr."

He held my gaze for several moments longer, and I refused to look away or blink. When he nodded finally, I detected a glimmer of respect in his dark eyes.

"You'd better practice your jumping," he said. "And those extra soldiers of yours, too. We make our move in three days."

TWENTY-THREE

SILK WHISPERED AROUND my ankles and diamonds lay cold on my neck and wrists as I paced the floor of the library, waiting for Adam, reviewing the steps of what must be done that night in my head. My stomach churned and my skin prickled. Tonight I was going to a gala.

A gala for a dictator.

The door opened, and Gabe slipped inside. "Lia—"

He caught sight of me.

"Oh," he said, and stopped in the doorway, whatever he was about to say forgotten.

Raven had helped me color my hair black with hair polish, and she'd lined my eyes with paints. The dress I wore was long and sleek, with a low back and strings of pearls that formed delicate sleeves on the edges of my shoulders. I wore borrowed jewelry, and it felt too hard against my skin. I was used to wool and string, not this strange mixture of soft and sharp that left me feeling vulnerable and wild at the same time.

"It's me," I said with a nervous laugh.

Gabe looked different, too. His hair was slicked back from his face. He wore an ankle-length black coat edged with gold thread and glittering buttons. Gloves covered his hands, and he held a silk hat in his left one. He was the biggest risk tonight—he could be recognized—but even Korr had agreed that he needed to be present for the coup, considering that he was one of the surviving members of the royal family. We'd have to keep him from being spotted by anyone who would know his face.

He looked magnificent, but upon closer observation, bruise-like shadows lined the places beneath his eyes, and tension pinched the skin between his eyebrows.

"When was the last time you slept?"

He made a noncommittal noise as he brushed my question aside. "I'll sleep when we've finished this."

The plan ran through my head on a continuous loop. I chewed my lip and went to the window. Below, steamcoaches lined the drive, waiting to carry us to the palace.

Gabe tapped the brim of his hat against his leg.

"You look stunning," he said after a moment. "Like Aeralian nobility."

My stomach twisted and clenched with sudden terror. I turned away from the glass and crossed to Gabe's side. "What if they all see right through me?"

"They won't. The plan's going to succeed," he said.

The library door opened again, and Adam entered. He noted our clasped hands.

"Ready?" His voice was terse.

"We're ready," I said, pulling my hands free.

Adam turned and went into the hallway without another word, and Gabe and I followed. Raven met us on the landing, dressed in purple velvet and wearing flowers in her hair. She took Adam's arm.

We walked in silence to the steamcoaches. There were three of them, black and glistening like they'd just emerged from the river. Steam rose from their engines and dissipated in the rain. Korr emerged from the house with Ann on his arm. He didn't speak to us, and we didn't speak to him. Any talk was superfluous at this point; we'd all rehearsed our parts in the plan until we could recite them backward in our dreams.

Korr handed Ann into the first steamcoach and climbed in after her. Gabe and I took the second, and Adam and Raven the third.

The inside of the steamcoach smelled like wet leather and cigars. I sank back against the seat and stared out the fogged window at the rain. The coach lurched, and we were heading toward the palace. My fingers knotted in my lap.

Gabe watched me from the opposite seat, a distant expression on his face. "Here we are again," he said, preternaturally calm. "About to face a future that might hold death or dismemberment. Nothing is certain between us, as usual. You look calm as a snow bank. And I'm about to tell you I love you."

I lifted my head.

Half of his mouth turned in a bitter smile. "But I know the rest of this story, don't I? You'll run off to have another adventure, and we'll be separated, and somewhere down the road we'll meet again and do it all over again." He paused and rubbed the space between his eyes. "When does it stop?"

"Gabe—"

"I know," he said. "This is hardly the time or the place."

The steamcoach stopped before I could reply, and my heart stopped with it. The doors opened, and a coachman handed us down onto a walk of paved marble. Light blazed around us, making diamonds out of the raindrops as they fell from the black sky. The palace ahead glowed, a sentinel against the storm. Gabe offered me his arm. I curled my fingers around his bicep, sucked in a breath of steamy, rain-soaked air, and stepped with him toward the palace.

Guards lined the covered walkway, their faces as still as if carved from stone. They held guns across their gleaming uniforms, and their eyes were covered with shades. In a flash of a memory I saw the Cages, the bars gleaming with ice, the air swirling with snowflakes, the perimeter just patches of gray trees, white snow, and blue snow blossoms. I felt the bite of the wind beneath my cloak, and shivers skittered down my spine. Then I was back in the present, surrounded by light and marble and the scent of rain and the heat of the steamcoaches, but the soldiers' attention lingered on me, and the sensation of being watched was the same.

Ahead of us, a line of nobles and dignitaries ascended steps into the palace. Hedges lined the steps to the palace entrance, all of them cut into sharp, straight lines.

"When my father owned this palace," Gabe murmured angrily, "those hedges blossomed. Now the Dictator has them cut down almost to nothing."

The interior of the palace was ornate, but an air of severity hung over the marble and delicate wrought iron. No rugs or furniture decorated the halls and vast foyer, and simple state flags hung from the balconies on the second and third stories of the hall. The structure echoed with the vastness of a long-empty tomb.

Gabe's jaw flexed.

Korr and Ann entered behind us, and a hush filled the room as people turned to look. Korr had a reputation. He dropped a low bow, acknowledging their notice of him as though it were reverence and not revulsion, then he strode toward the main ballroom with Ann at his side. I almost missed the sidelong glance he gave her as they entered the ballroom. His gaze was naked, vulnerable, as if he were seeking her support for the arduous task ahead.

Adam and Raven didn't look at us as they followed Korr and Ann to the main ballroom along with the other guests.

Gabe and I drifted toward one of the side doors. We had a device to find, and not much time to do it.

"This way," Gabe whispered, and together we slipped through the crowd toward the far wall of the room. We reached a door half-hidden behind a banner, and Gabe eased it open as I stood in front of him, pretending to adjust my flowing skirt. He grabbed my wrist, and I slid behind the banner and joined him in a narrow corridor, much plainer than the grand entryway we'd just exited. Wood panels lined the ceiling and walls. The hum of the crowd's conversation snapped to a murmur as he shut the door behind us.

"This is a servants' hall," he explained. "I used to hide here to escape my lessons when I was small. Cat was the first one who showed it to me. It will lead us downstairs to the basement level."

We descended a spiraling set of stairs and reached a landing. I stopped in astonishment. Another hall intersected with the one we'd just exited, this one wider and made of stone. Dozens of doors and staircases, large and small, spun away in all directions, a maze of steps and shapes.

"The main artery, they called it," Gabe said wistfully. "This place used to bustle with activity. Servants carrying trays and blankets and messages back and forth." He shook his head and glanced around. "This way."

He stopped at a place between two doors and pulled back a panel, revealing a door that led to another staircase, this one so narrow we could only walk single-file down the steps. "This one's a secret. I imagine even the Dictator's guards don't know about it. The story goes that a prince had them built so he could sneak down to the basement without anyone knowing—not even the servants."

"Why didn't he want anyone to know?" I asked.

Gabe shrugged. "The legend claims that he harbored a secret affinity for murdering people."

"Oh," I said.

"We should hurry. The Dictator must be making his speech now. We don't have much time. This way is longer, but we'll bypass the guards."

I followed him down the staircase. The temperature changed as we descended, and the air became colder and damper. The gaslight was dimmer here. I heard music far away, sounds of the party. The smell of dust and dampness wafted toward us.

The stairs ended in a dark corridor. Gabe went first. We crept around a corner and entered a room lined with shelves.

"Where are we now?" I whispered.

"The archive room."

Borde had drawn us a picture of what the Alice device looked like. It was cylindrical, similar to the PLD but thinner, longer, and with more mechanical knobs on the sides. It's appearance was alien, insect-like.

We dug through piles of faded and papers and rusted artifacts. I uncovered dozens of odd-looking curiosities, but nothing that matched the image Borde had sketched for us.

Defeat swamped me. "It isn't here."

"Wait," Gabe said, turning from the shelves to face the way we'd come. "There's another chamber in here, I remember. Maybe they have the device there. Come on."

We went back into the corridor. This time, Gabe stopped halfway to the servants' landing and tapped on a wall.

"Here," he said, and pushed inward.

The panel gave way, revealing another room just as he'd promised. This one was smaller, with just as many shelves, each of them crammed with books and papers. On a table in the center of the room lay a spread of strange and wonderful instruments.

My stomach dropped at what I saw.

Among them was the Alice device.

"Gabe," I said, my voice coming out in a strangled whisper. "There it is."

A voice spoke behind us. "I was wondering when you would show up."

I snatched up the device and turned as a figure wearing an eye patch stepped from the shadows in the corridor outside and into the dim light of the chamber. Gabe started in astonishment.

"Cat?"

A slight smile touched his friend's mouth. "I thought I'd find you here, friend. This was our old haunt, was it not?"

"You aren't supposed to be part of this mission," Gabe said.

"I couldn't leave you to do it alone," Cat said. "This was our place. We always came here together. I didn't want that to change." His gaze fell on the cylindrical metal piece in my hands, and he sighed. "Good, you've found the Alice device. Come on, we have to hurry. There isn't much time left."

We followed him out to the stairs. Cat moved swiftly, not stopping until he'd reached the Artery. There he paused and listened.

"They're in the ballroom now," he said. "This way. It shouldn't be long."

We took a different corridor than the one Gabe and I had entered through, heading toward the sounds of the crowd. My heart thudded and my chest squeezed. I stared at the back of Cat's head. A thought tingled at the back of my mind, and I grabbed Gabe's arm and pulled him back.

"Gabe," I whispered harshly. "We never told Cat about the Alice device. He never knew its name."

"What?" Gabe's eyebrows drew together as he turned his head toward me.

"The device. How did he know about it? He called it Alice."

Gabe turned toward Cat, his mouth dropping open. Cat paused and looked back at us.

"Come on," he said. "We have to hurry."

"Wait," I said. "I think we should talk first."

Cat's visible eye hardened slightly. "There isn't time for that."

"How did you hear about the Alice device?" I demanded. "We never mentioned it to you. Only a select number of people knew, and you were not among them."

"Adam told me."

"You're lying." I took a step closer to him.

That was when Cat drew the gun from his coat.

TWENTY-FOUR

"WHAT ARE YOU doing?" Gabe yelped as Cat pointed the weapon straight at my chest. "Cat! What—?"

"Shut up," Cat said. "Both of you are going to listen to me, and listen well. You're going to hand me that device, you're going to march out this door and into that ballroom, and you aren't going to do or say anything."

"*You're* the traitor," I said as understanding dawned. "You're the one who was leaking information. Not Claire."

"How astute," he drawled. "You should be an investigator, Frost dweller." The muzzle of his gun glinted in the dim light as he waved it. "Now give me the device."

"Cat," Gabe said. His voice was a broken whisper. "Why? We...we're friends. You're like a brother to me."

"We were never brothers," Cat said. "I was a servant and you were a master. I never forgot that."

"I don't understand—"

"I'm sorry," Cat said. "This is how it has to be. You can't help who you are, Gabe, but that doesn't change what I have to do because of who I am, and who I plan to be. If I can thwart your revolution, I can make a name for myself. If I help you, I'm nothing. Just another ex-servant lost in a cause bigger than himself, wondering how long before you throw me away—the way you threw away Clara."

Gabe gasped at the mention of her. His eyes were black with pain.

"I didn't—"

"Save your protests," Cat said. "I don't want to hear them."

My palms were slick with sweat. My heart pounded painfully. My mind was screaming for me to do something. He was going to ruin the plan. The revolution would fail. We would be captured. We would all be executed. Jonn and Ivy would die.

"The device," Cat said.

My heart ripped in two as I extended it toward him. He wrenched it from my fingers and shoved it into the pocket of his coat.

"Now move," he said.

Gabe's face was the color of ash. He joined me as I stepped toward the door, my mind spinning with plans. Perhaps if I spun and smashed the gun from his hand. Perhaps if I ran. Perhaps...

"Not a word," Cat snapped, "or I won't hesitate to—"

A stone bust of the Dictator swung from the shadows and connected with Cat's skull. He dropped like a sack of turnips, and I leapt for his gun. Clutching it, I scrambled up and pointed the weapon at whoever had just knocked our captor out.

Red hair. Startled eyes. Skinny face.

"Clara?" Gabe stuttered.

She set the bust down with a thump and blew a strand of hair from her forehead. "I didn't think I was going to make it in time. You're pretty lucky I did."

"What are you doing here?" I lowered the weapon slowly. "How did you know?"

She shrugged delicately. "After Gabe kicked me out for being a spy, I knew *I* wasn't the spy, but he was right about someone leaking information. The evidence was there. So, I did some investigating of my own. Turns out, our friend Cat here makes regular trips into the Prison District to play cards with the guards. He took one such trip just before your friend's excavation was raided by soldiers and that device confiscated. It didn't take me more than two seconds to figure out what was going on."

We stared down at Cat's unconscious body. Gabe rubbed a hand over his eyes. "So it was Cat. I can't believe it."

"I have never betrayed you, Gabe." Clara took his hands with hers and tipped her head so she was looking into his face. "Never. You can check the records. My family was always loyal."

"How did you know?" he stuttered.

"I overheard you asking Lia to find the records, and it wasn't hard to guess what you were after. You wanted to know if it was my family who betrayed you, who caused your arrest. It wasn't." She withdrew a paper from her coat and threw it down. "I found the records myself. Look. It's been Cat all along." She glanced at him. "I suggest we tie him up."

I crouched down and pulled the device from Cat's pocket. Cradling it close, I stood and moved to Gabe's side before tucking it into my pocket, the one closest to my heart. I pulled ribbons from my hair and bound Cat's hands and feet.

While I worked, Gabe picked up the paper and turned it over slowly, as if any quick movements might cause it to disintegrate into dust. His eyebrows pinched together as he read.

"Now come on, we have to hurry," Clara said. "There isn't much time." She strode down the corridor without waiting for us.

Gabe and I exchanged a glance. He slipped the paper into his pocket, and we hurried after her.

The ballroom retained some of its vestiges of the old glory days. Gold-gilded chandeliers illuminated arching ceilings and walls hung with intricate tapestries depicting Aeralis's history. One caught my eye—it showed a great battle of fire and blood, with gleaming white buildings like I'd seen in the Compound being destroyed by ships from the sky.

The Dictator sat on a dais at the far end of the room, flanked by several of his officers and a few soldiers in gleaming gray and brass. He was younger than I'd imagined, and handsome, with a mouth full of sharp teeth that glittered in the light of the chandeliers as he smiled. Above the dais hung a massive clock, the one decorative element in the room. The hands glimmered faintly in the gaslight. In five more minutes, the clock would strike ten, and we would make our move. We couldn't delay any later than that. Everything had to be timed perfectly, or the people coming through the gate wouldn't be able to complete the jump.

Korr stood near the Dictator, his chin high and his expression unreadable. He spotted me in the crowd and raised his eyebrows. I nodded slightly to let him know that we'd been successful. We had the device.

Korr said something to the Dictator. He had one hand on his pocket, where the device was located. I couldn't take my eyes off it. My throat was dry. My skin prickled with sweat. I edged along the crowd, trying to get closer to Adam and Raven.

A clatter of feet rang out, and a voice cut through the hum of the crowd.

"Stop!"

My stomach plummeted as Cat staggered into the ballroom, accompanied by a soldier. A trickle of blood dripped down his forehead, and his wrists were red and raw where his ropes had been. His eyes swung around the room and fixed on the Dictator.

Heads turned. People murmured. A hush fell over the proceedings.

"Your Eminence," Cat gasped. "There are traitors in this room plotting to take Aeralis from you!"

Korr stilled. At various points around the room, I saw Ann, Raven, and Adam freeze. All eyes were on Cat.

"Who is this?" the Dictator demanded, rising from his chair.

"I work in your intelligence unit," Cat managed. "Your Eminence, Prince Gabriel is here in this room right now. He and his friends knocked me out and tied me up when I tried to stop him, and I just managed to get free."

The Dictator smiled. It looked like a snarl. "The prince is dead," he said. "You speak lies."

"He is here," Cat insisted. He turned a wild circle and caught sight of Gabe. "There he is!"

The crowd withdrew as soldiers closed around us. One pushed me to my knees, and I heard the click of a gun near my ear. Two of them seized Gabe's arms.

The Dictator curled his fingers in a command to bring him closer, and the soldiers forced Gabe forward into the middle of the room and pushed him to his knees. One pressed a gun to his head.

Korr didn't move from his place beside the dais. His hand tightened around his glass, and his lips whitened as he stared at his brother on the floor.

I couldn't breathe. The plan could continue without Gabe. He was not the heir. Would Korr sacrifice him to save the revolution?

"There are other traitors here," Cat said. "Her," he said, pointing to Raven. "And him." He pointed at Adam.

Soldiers flanked them and dragged them forward. Adam didn't struggle as one guard struck him in the face. When he turned his face back, blood ran from his nose.

The Dictator surveyed them without comment and turned back to Gabe. He paced a circle around him, hands clasped behind his back. Instead of losing his temper, he laughed.

"Korr," the Dictator said, turning to face the nobleman. "It seems your brother is alive. What a surprise, eh?"

"Half-brother," Korr said. His smirked faintly, but his eyes were cold and hard.

"What should we do about this?" the Dictator asked.

It was a test. Cat couldn't denounce Korr—he didn't know the nobleman was involved—but if Korr tried to save Gabe's life, his own would be lost.

"Kill him," Korr said. "Of course."

Gabe kept his eyes fixed on his brother's face. His expression never changed.

I saw a movement at the edge of the crowd. Clara. She pressed a hand over her mouth at the scene before her— Gabe on the ground, weapons trained on him, Korr's impassive face.

"And how should I do that?" the Dictator mused. "A bullet to the head?"

"Too messy," Korr said. "You'll ruin the party. Besides, you should do something dramatic. Make an example of him."

The Dictator smirked, and I realized where Korr had learned that particular expression. "Do you have any ideas?"

Korr withdrew the PLD from his pocket.

We had one minute remaining before the jump time. One minute before everything would be lost. My heart beat so hard I could hear it. Nausea crawled in my throat.

"I obtained this in the Frost," Korr said. "It's that device I was seeking, the one with great power. The one only I believed was important. Do you remember?"

"Yes, yes," the Dictator said, with a tone of boredom creeping into his voice. "You and your devices. It is real. You are vindicated."

"It's a portal," Korr said. "Let's send the prince through it."

The Dictator tipped his head to one side, suddenly interested. "Where does this portal lead?"

Korr's mouth twisted in a wry smile. "Somewhere truly, wretchedly horrific."

"How delightful," the Dictator said.

Korr crouched down to one knee and unfolded the device.

Thirty seconds before jump time.

I clenched my fingers so tightly that they went numb. My nails dug into my palms.

Korr activated the device.

Blue light shot up from the PLD and filled the ballroom. The people screamed and trembled. The soldiers wavered in their places beside the Dictator as crackles of energy radiated out like lightning, forming a circle.

The Dictator's face was ghoulish in the glow. He surveyed the effect of the PLD with delight.

"Throw him in," he said. "But first—" He looked at the soldier who had the gun to Gabe's head. "First make sure he won't ever come back."

Horror blossomed on Korr's face. He threw himself forward against his brother, knocking Gabe aside just as the soldier fired. Gabe skidded across the floor. Korr fell to the ground, one hand clutched to his side and blood seeping through his fingers. The Dictator's expression twisted in something ugly as understanding dawned.

"You," he shouted at Korr. "Traitor!"

That was when the clock struck ten.

The blue rippled and stretched, and then Restorationists and Wanderers were streaming through it side by side, guns in hand. The room erupted in chaos. Gunfire echoed through the room. The soldiers whirled in confusion. Raven disarmed the man guarding her with one well-placed elbow to his face while he gaped at the PLD in astonishment. Adam leaped to his feet and grabbed Cat, holding him in a chokehold. Guests in silk and velvet fled screaming into the halls before Korr's men managed to shut the doors to the ballroom.

I found my way to Gabe and dragged him to his feet.

"Are you all right?"

He pushed my hands away. "Where's Korr?"

"I don't know. Come on, we have to move before—"

Gabe spotted his brother's crumpled form and broke away from me, running toward Korr as a roar split the air. Three Watchers surged through the blue vortex of light and into the room. They opened their jaws and snarled at the soldiers, who threw down their weapons and dropped to their knees. They'd heard the stories. They knew their guns would do nothing.

The Dictator turned and ran. Gabe saw him and stopped.

"Lia, there's a secret door behind the dais," Gabe shouted. "He's heading for it!"

I wrenched my long skirt away from my ankles and ran after him. He skidded on the tile as he reached the platform, and I leaped after him. I seized the end of his gold-trimmed coat and yanked. He fell hard, and I fell with him.

One of the Wanderers grabbed the Dictator and forced his hands behind his back before he could try to run again. It was Stone. Two growling Watchers flanked us, their eyes glowing and their tails lashing. I gazed at them and marveled that my sister had been right when she'd promised me that the Watchers would do her bidding and make the leap through the gate to help us.

"Please," the Dictator panted. "Don't let them eat me."

"You won't be so lucky," Stone hissed.

I got to my feet and looked around.

The Dictator was secured. The sharp retort of gunfire came from the halls, but I knew it wouldn't be long before those men surrendered.

Adam and Raven joined several of their fellow agents in collecting weapons. The Watchers paced in the center of the room.

Gabe spotted Korr, crumpled on the floor beside the PLD, blood streaming through his fingers. He rushed to his brother's side. Ann was there already, supporting Korr's head.

One of the Restorationists climbed onto the dais and addressed the terrified crowd.

"Tonight we return Aeralis to its rightful ruler," he shouted. "Tonight we see the monarchy restored."

A hush filled the room, punctuated only by the sound of the Watchers hissing and Gabe repeating Korr's name. Then, the crowd began to cheer.

But all I could see was Gabe's anguished face as his brother took his last breath.

TWENTY-FIVE

PAIN TWISTED INSIDE me at the sight of Gabe's grief, but I couldn't stay. This was the part of the plan that depended on me. I had to get through the portal and bring the Alice device to Gordon.

I fell through the portal and into darkness. Icy wind swirled around me, tugging at my hair and clothes. I slammed into the ground on the other side. Echlos.

I struggled to my feet, and hands grabbed me.

"You have it?" Borde's voice trembled with excitement.

I dug in my pocket for the device, still blinking from the effects of the jump. Borde snatched it from my fingers and crooned to it as if it were a baby.

"Let's go," he said. "There are horses outside."

He held a bag that contained the flares Gordon had given me, along with ropes to restrain him once he'd handed over the cure. Together we rushed for the exterior, and the horses.

The ride through the Frost was a blur. We were so close. My hands trembled from exhaustion. So much had already happened already, but it wasn't over yet.

The clearing was empty and hushed with fresh-fallen snow when we reached it. I struck the flare against a rock, and it sent a column of red-colored smoke and light into the sky and bathed the trees around us in a blood-colored glow. I dropped it and let it burn as we waited. Borde slipped into the bushes to hide. I stood alone in the clearing.

Minutes or hours passed. Finally, the faint *crunch, crunch* of footsteps met my straining ears. I turned.

Gordon.

I held the device in my hands, palms out, like a waiting supplicant. Gordon stepped forward and regarded me, then the object in my hands.

"You found it," he said. "I didn't expect that you would."

"No faith in me?"

He didn't answer. He surveyed the shadows a moment, and my heart skipped a beat.

He reached out and took the device. "It's real," he said.

"Yes. Now give me the cure."

The forest rustled around us. Somewhere close, I heard the faint snarl of a Watcher. A twig snapped. Gordon whirled, staring at the bushes where Borde crouched in hiding. His chest rose and fell.

"You didn't come alone. You have a weapon here. They're attracted to them, I know."

Borde stood and pointed the gun at Gordon's chest. "Give us the cure," he said. "We've given you what you want."

Gordon stared at Borde. "Meridus," he snarled. "I should have known you'd try to interfere. This time, I'm not going to let you."

"Refuse and I'll put a bullet in your leg," Borde said.

Gordon started toward the older man, but the latter waved the gun warningly, and he stopped.

Borde backed up, holding the gun steady. "Get us what you promised. Slowly now."

Gordon feigned left and lunged forward, seizing the barrel of the gun. They struggled, and Borde slipped on the snow. The gun went off, and all the air left my lungs as the forest around me fell silent, a gasp of air and snow and trees all together at the shock of the sound.

Gordon toppled into the snow and lay still.

I screamed. The sound ripped from me. I was crying. My cheeks were wet; my hands were wet. I was running, sliding in the snow, turning him over. He was unmoving as I shook him.

He couldn't be dead.

"Lia," Borde said, touching my shoulder. "He's gone."

My breath was a squeak of anguish in my lungs. "No," I whispered. "No."

~

Our trip to the village was a blur. Trees spun around me. The cold licked straight to my bones and froze the skin on my face. I clung to the reins of my mount, my desperation a chant in my head.

Finally, the Farther-built walls of Iceliss shimmered in the distance, bathed in starlight and frosted with dried snow blossoms. Lights glowed in the windows of the houses, scattering steaks of warmth across the icy streets.

Jonn lay unmoving on the bed when we reached his room.

I fell on my knees beside him and picked up his hand. His fingers were cold. His chest didn't rise or fall. Tears began to gather in my eyes, my libation of sorrow. I clutched at his shirt, shaking him. "Jonn!"

"He's here," the Healer said, putting one hand on my shoulder. "He's just in a deep sleep."

I sat back, exhausted. "Where's my sister?"

I found her sleeping, too. She must have returned, exhausted, after sending the Watchers through the gate. Her skin had begun to turn sallow, and she didn't stir as I sank down beside her on the bed and stroked her hair. I saw Gordon's final moments in my mind, his shoulders going slack and his legs sagging before he dropped like a doll. I kept petting her hair, the movements mechanical. I didn't know what else to do.

My sister opened her eyes. "Lia?" she mumbled, the word thick with sleep. "You're here?"

"I'm here," I said. My eyes clouded with tears again. "I thought you'd slipped into the coma."

"You're crying." She sat up and touched my shoulder. I turned my head away so she couldn't see the moisture betraying me. "What is it? You never cry. Lia?"

I shook my head. I couldn't tell her, not yet. I couldn't bear to speak the words.

"Oh," she said, straightening. "The raccoon."

"Did it die?" I asked it wearily.

"No." Her face brightened as she spoke. "He's recovered completely. He didn't even go through the coughing phase that usually occurs when healing from the Sickness. He's a strong little guy, I suppose."

My hand paused. "What?"

"The raccoon is well. The healers said it was nothing short of miraculous. I think it shows what a little love can do."

The most fragile tendril of hope unfurled in me. My lungs heaved as I straightened. I moved my lips, but nothing came out. The raccoon was healed. Something had happened to it. Memories scratched at the back of my mind, begging to be unleashed. What had happened to it?

Ivy was still rambling about the animal, oblivious to my change of mood. "He's a cheerful little thing. Loves biscuits. He—"

"Not that," I interrupted. "What happened to the raccoon last week, Ivy?"

She stared at me, puzzled. "He was in a cage? I cared for him."

"No, no. He was injured somehow. How was he injured?"

"Oh, a mothkat bit him. But it didn't seem to hurt him. In fact—"

I was already running for the door.

~

The wind whipped at my hair and cloak as I ran down the path. Snow blossoms brushed my ankles, their petals luminous in the moonlight.

I needed to find a mothkat.

I spotted a rotting hollow tree trunk at the edge of the path and peered inside. Gleaming eyes winked back at me. Mothkats. I took off my cloak and stretched it over the opening, then kicked the tree. A few creatures flew out and thrashed against the fabric, trying to get free, and I scooped them up and held the opening of my makeshift bag shut with both hands. I turned back toward the village, running again.

Borde waited for me in Jonn's room, Ivy and one of the Healers at his side.

"Mothkats," I managed. "One bit the raccoon, and now it's better. Maybe if they bite Jonn and Ivy..."

"It's worth trying," the Healer said.

I delivered the mothkats and stepped back. My stomach was rioting in terror. My lips were numb. The Healer pulled one of the mothkats from my cloak, and the creature squeaked and flopped in his hands as he carried it to my brother's bed.

Borde rolled up one of Jonn's sleeves and rubbed the arm with brandy to clean it.

I sank down beside my brother and dragged in a strangled breath as the Healer picked up Jonn's arm, which was bare to the elbow and glistening from the brandy. As I watched, he held the mothkat to the skin. The vermin thrashed, then sank its tiny mouth into Jonn's flesh. My brother moaned in his sleep. The Healer withdrew the mothkat and looked at Ivy.

"You next," he said.

She extended her arm and endured the bite without making a sound.

"Now what?" I asked.

"Now," he said, "we wait."

TWENTY-SIX

RAIN BLANKETED THE city of Astralux in gray. I stood in the conservatory of Korr's house, watching the droplets stream down the walls of glass and make pebbled shadows over the flowers and leaves inside the greenhouse. It was a grim day to celebrate the official reinstatement of the monarchy, an appropriate day to bury Korr.

The sound of a shovel filled the room. Gabe stood beside me, his face stiff as a mask, and I reached out and took Gabe's hand. I squeezed his fingers, but he didn't return the gesture. At Gabe's other side stood Ann, holding an urn, her expression remote and her eyes soft. I watched as a tear slipped down her cheek. We hadn't yet had an opportunity to speak alone, and we wouldn't, not until things here were finished. She'd been busy settling matters for Korr, wishes he'd expressed to her and no one else. Raven confided to me that Korr had left her the house and grounds, too. Ann had been swamped with details, and by the looks of her, unable to process what had happened yet.

When the servant finished digging a hole in the ground, Gabe stepped forward and lifted a bush covered in white blossoms. He placed it in the hole. Ann joined him and spilled the contents of the urn around the roots of the plant.

Korr's ashes.

"He wanted this," Ann said quietly, her voice barely audible above the rain. "He wanted to be absorbed into something beautiful when he died. He wanted to be part of something that wasn't pain and sorrow."

"He's part of more than he realizes," Gabe said. "He saved my life, and I will not waste what he's given me."

Much had happened in the last several days. After the palace had been seized and the Dictator imprisoned, word spread quickly through the city. The majority of the soldiers in the Dictator's employ willingly surrendered, and the city was immediate and enthusiastic in voicing their support of Gabe's return. Now, search for his cousin—the heir to the throne—was underway.

After the funeral was over, I stood uselessly as the crowd swirled around me. Political advisors swarmed Gabe, and a servant pulled Ann away to discuss another matter regarding the house.

I descended to the basement alone to where Borde had once again rigged the PLD to a power source to allow it to operate continuously. I needed to visit Jonn and Ivy. I needed to see for myself that they were well.

Steeling myself for the sickening fall and the swirl of gray, I stepped forward, and then I was spinning, careening through space until I struck a hard surface.

I lifted my head. Nausea swam through my veins, but I staggered up and headed for the village. As Borde had promised, each trip got easier.

As Iceliss swung into view, I stopped and inhaled a breath of pine-scented air. I looked at Iceliss now and saw what it had been hundreds of years earlier, and I saw what it was now. A small, tired, worn village of stone in the middle of a world of ice and white. But it was brave, a tenacious barnacle clinging to the landscape, refusing to be forever scraped away by hardship or occupation or internal strife.

My feet found the path to the gate. As I passed beneath the bars that enclosed the path, the cold and ever-present reminder of our painful past, I stopped and put one hand against the metal. It was good metal. Ideas filled my head, visions of future projects. We could build houses with this metal, greenhouses, a bigger school. Something bright and warm nestled inside my chest. Hope.

We actually had a future, and my siblings would live in it.

I hurried to the Mayor's house on the top of the hill. As I reached the porch, I stopped. Jonn sat on a chair, wrapped in quilts and facing the forest. The wind caught his hair and made it dance. As he turned and caught sight of me, he smiled.

A sharp ache filled me, the feeling that I'd almost broken something precious and irreplaceable, but had caught it right before it hit the ground. I trembled, overcome with sudden fear and relief mingled together. I took a deep breath and approached him.

"You're up. Are you strong enough to be outside in the cold?"

"They couldn't keep me in bed any longer," he said. His voice was rusty from disuse, but it was strong. The dark shadows under his eyes were fading, and his color was returning.

"How are things in Aeralis?" he asked quietly.

"Progressing." I thought about the complexities of what would happen next for Gabe, for all of them. "They're looking for the heir now, but if he isn't found..." I sighed. "Gabe will be king."

Jonn nodded thoughtfully, and we were both silent for a moment.

"Ivy told me," he said finally. "About Aaron. About who our da really was."

I rubbed my forehead. I didn't have much to say on the subject.

"What about Borde?" he asked after the silence grew almost too strong. "Is he planning to stay?"

"Borde leaves soon," I said. "He's planning to travel back to his time before nightfall."

"Our father...?"

I swallowed hard. "I have no idea what he's planning to do."

"No." Jonn leaned forward in the chair, straining to see. "Look. I think it's our father. He looks like us."

I turned.

Aaron stood at the entrance to the front garden, his hand on the fence. The wind stirred his hair and made the ends of his Aeralian-styled coat flutter in the wind.

"Yes, that's him." A mixture of emotions filled me. He was here. He'd come.

When he saw that we'd noticed him, Aaron approached the house.

"Aaron," I said, greeting him and warning him at the same time, but he didn't seem to hear me. He stared at Jonn as if seeing color for the first time. "You look like my father," he managed after an unbearably long pause.

"And clearly, I look like my father," Jonn replied evenly.

Aaron blanched at hearing the word *father* from his son's mouth. His gaze flicked over Jonn, taking in the chair, the blanket. "You are well?"

"I'm recovering," Jonn said. His tone was more cautious than cool.

The door opened, and Ivy emerged. "Lia!" She caught sight of Aaron and paused. "Who are you?"

Aaron was speechless.

"Aaron," I said. "This is Ivy. Ivy, this is, well, this is Aaron."

"You're our father," she guessed.

He nodded.

They looked at each other, father and daughter, neither quite able to find anything to say. Finally, Aaron stammered, "You look so much like her."

"My mother?" Ivy asked.

"Your sister," he said.

Ivy's face blossomed in a shy smile.

We were all quiet. Jonn looked torn between wanting to interrogate Aaron and embrace him. Aaron shifted his feet.

"How did you find us here?" I asked, interrupting the uncomfortable pause.

Aaron glanced at me, looking relieved to have a question asked that he could easily answer. "I did not come alone. Some of the others accompanied me...Adam, Ann, Gabe."

I needed to see them, and I was not sorry to escape this scene either.

"I'll be back later," I murmured, and slipped away, leaving them to their stilted conversation. My heart was still torn. I didn't want a replacement for the da I'd known. But Aaron was here, he was my father, and that mattered to me more than I'd realized. I had many other things to parcel out at the moment. I'd make peace with my father's presence in time, as would my siblings.

I wandered through Iceliss, looking for the others. I saw no sign of them.

I realized where they must be, and I passed through the gate and headed for my family's farm. The sound of my feet was just a whisper against the path. The wind caught my cloak and flung it behind me, and I ran. Snowflakes drifted around me, bits of white like a shower of petals at a wedding. The sky glowed above me, blue as hope and bright as love, the same color as the snow blossoms that lined the trail through the wilderness of silver and white.

Here and there, green punctuated the snow where plants pushed through the crust of ice and reached for the sun.

I reached the hill that looked down over the farm, and I caught my breath. There were the charred remains of the house and the barn, there were the paddock and the yard. There was the tree where I'd hung the lantern for Adam. The sight of the blackened boards was somehow cleansing. The old was gone, but I would build it again. I would make something new, something better.

Footprints led though the yard. I followed them.

The old Watcher ward clattered in the wind above the door as I knocked my boots against the remains of the threshold and stepped onto the charred foundation of the house. I caught sight of Ann at the fireplace, waiting.

"Ann," I breathed.

She ran to me, and I hugged her as she clung to me fiercely and sobbed. I ached to be able to take even a sliver of her pain and hold it in my heart instead, but all I could do was stand with her. She was hot and damp from weeping, and as she held onto me, something deep uncorked inside me, and I cried, too. I wept for my parents, for the burned farm, for all the people we'd lost during the past year. We swayed together, our shared grief a dance of friendship.

Finally, Ann drew back and wiped her eyes. "It's good to be back home," she said. "It's easier to process it here, somehow."

"The Frost does that," I said. "It's clean and uncluttered."

Ann nodded and gazed at the open sky above us, where snowflakes were fluttering in the wind. "This house..." she said. "I'm so sorry, Lia."

"I'll rebuild it," I said firmly.

She nodded and rubbed her hand over my arm. "Gabe is looking for you," she said. "He and Adam came with me, and they both wanted to speak with you. Did you see them?"

"I did not." I bit my lip and looked toward the door.

"You should go find Gabe," she said. "Borde is going to close the gate soon, and there isn't much time."

"I'll be back," I promised her, and then I left the house.

I knew where he was.

One wall of the barn still stood, and near it, the secret door to the room below the barn floor gaped like an open mouth. I descended into the darkness, and it was quiet and warm inside. Sunlight striped the floor where it leaked through the cracks. The air smelled of ash and soot. Most of the things inside were burned.

"Gabe?"

He stepped out of the darkness. His hands found me, and I embraced him back, holding him in his pain. I rubbed his back with my hands, and he sighed.

"Look at this place," he muttered.

I said nothing. I just put my head on his shoulder.

"He's dead," Gabe said, speaking of Korr.

I nodded against his shoulder.

"I miss him," he said. "How absurd. We were barely civil to each other, and yet now that he's dead I'm breaking apart inside."

"You were brothers," I said.

"Half-brothers." He laughed, low and sad, and shook his head. "No, just brothers."

"You loved him," I said. "You can't help but love family." I thought of Aaron, and was quiet.

Gabe pulled away and looked into my face as if just remembering at the word *family*. "How is Jonn? Ivy?"

"They are well," I said. "Recovering. The Healers say Jonn will not get his health back as he'd hoped, though, not since he had intervention to cure the Sickness rather than mutation from the Sickness changing his body. He'll still have a withered leg."

"He's no less of a man for it," Gabe said. "It doesn't weaken him or strengthen him. It is simply part of who he is."

I nodded. But would Jonn see it that way? I hoped so.

"What about Cat?" I asked.

Gabe winced at the mention of his friend. "He is currently in prison with the rest of the Dictator's men. I don't know what to do with him. Nothing hurts like the prospect of punishing those you care about, but he betrayed us. Not just of me, but of our country."

"And Clara?"

"You used her name," he said, with a hint of a smile.

I shrugged.

"She is well. She sends her regards."

"I'm glad to hear it."

"Lia," Gabe said, and his voice changed into something half hopeful, half fearful. "I must go soon. I have duties in Aeralis, many duties, but I wanted to speak with you."

My stomach knotted. I was still as I listened.

Gabe twisted his hands together. "Much has happened between us over the last few months," he continued. "We have been forced apart, brought back together. Things have changed. I...I know we have not always agreed, and we have not always had the same ideas about things. We've both changed. But..."

I couldn't breathe as I waited for him to continue.

"I want you to come back with me," he said.

"Come back with you?"

"To Aeralis. I want you to stay there for good," Gabe said.

"I am done working for causes—"

"You misunderstand me," he interrupted. "I'm asking you to marry me, Lia." His voice softened. "Marry me? I want your answer now. I need it now. Lia, please."

Silence hummed through the bark, broken only by the flutter of chicken wings.

I didn't speak. I couldn't.

His eyes darkened at my hesitation. "Don't spare my feelings because of my brother's recent passing," he said.

I took a deep breath. "I can't."

Gabe shoved one hand through his hair. His mouth twisted with pain. "Why not? Is it *him*?" He didn't say Adam.

"No. The Frost is my home," I said. "I cannot leave it. Not now. You have duties in Aeralis, as you said. I have duties here. I'm a Weaver, and I'm woven into the history and future of this place as deeply as it is in me. I have Jonn, Ivy, Ann, and yes, Adam."

He made a slight gesture with his hand, almost as if he wanted to touch me but he lacked the courage. When he raised his eyes to mine, they brimmed with regret. "I loved you, Lia. How did I let you slip away from me?"

"That isn't what happened." I said it gently, yet every word felt like broken glass on my tongue.

"I love you still." His face was drawn with hurt, confusion.

"I know," I said. "I don't think you believe it, but I love you still, too."

"And yet you love him."

It wasn't a question, and I couldn't deny it.

"I do."

He made a sound of pain deep in his throat.

"Wait. Please listen." I considered my words. I'd thought about them a great deal. "It is possible to love two people. In fact, I love many people. I love Jonn and Ann and Ivy, and many others. Romantic love is different in some ways, but in many, many other ways, it is much the same. I loved you, Gabe. I love you still. You must know that. I didn't mean it to happen this way, but it did."

He laughed, low and sad. "You may love me, but you didn't choose me."

I winced. *Choose.* As if he were a spoon on a shelf, and I had picked him up and examined his merits and flaws before putting him back. Were the beauty and terror of living and loving as crass as that? Could it be that simple?

"Gabe." I touched his hand, and his fingers were cold against mine. "You were the one who inspired me to put myself back together when I thought I was broken. You were the one who challenged me to look beyond my fear and insularity to see a world outside my own. Love makes weavers of us all—and you're sewn into the tapestry of my life."

Gabe's shoulders rose and fell as he sighed. "So this is goodbye."

"It is," I said. "But I will see you again."

It was a promise.

Our final embrace was too short, and then he was gone, leaving me alone in the room beneath barn floor, hurting and whole at the same time, filled with sadness and assurance that I'd made the right choice.

I climbed out and stepped into the snow. The air smelled of snow blossoms. I walked into the wild without direction, following the sound of bluewings singing songs of comfort to the wind, thinking.

A branch snapped to my left, and I stopped.

Adam.

His expression was guarded. "Lia."

"I've just been speaking to Gabe," I said.

Something flickered in his dark eyes. He turned his head to the side, hiding his expression, but not before I caught a glimpse of his pain. "I'm glad you found him. He was looking for you. It seemed urgent."

"Yes," I agreed. "He had something to ask me."

Adam looked at me again.

"He asked me to marry him," I admitted.

He lowered his head. "When do you leave for Astralux?"

"Adam," I said.

He looked at me.

I look a deep breath. "When you are with me," I said. "I feel as though I can breathe again."

Adam stilled.

"I don't have any polished poetry to recite for you," I continued, and took a step toward him. "I just want to see you safe and happy...everything and everyone you love safe and happy."

"Lia," Adam said, his voice strained. He took one of my hands and pulled me to him.

I put a finger to his lips. "Don't try to explain yourself," I whispered. "Not yet. I only wanted to communicate my own position on the matter."

Then I kissed him, and he tasted like home and goodness and everything that was beautiful.

EPILOGUE

BORDE LEFT US that evening, after congratulating Adam and I on our engagement. He said he was heading into the past to fix something that had gone awry. I slipped Ivy's journal in among his things, and I suppose he threw it into a garbage bin accidentally, where he would find it later in his own future. I didn't tell him, because some things make beautiful secrets.

Adam and I were married several months later, in the height of summer, when the snow blossoms covered the forest in blue and the snow melted into muddy patches along the paths. Adam took my name—Weaver—and we reclaimed my family's farm and made our home there. Gabe broke his silence with me to send a wedding present—materials for a greenhouse. We built it in the yard behind the house, and I filled it with flowers. It soon became my favorite place to me, for in it I felt close to Gabe and Aeralis, but I could still see my beloved Frost through the glass.

The Wanderers chose to stay in Aeralis, and they left the Frost for good and were welcomed for their part in the revolution. Stone and I still saw each other occasionally, though, as he came to visit the wilderness from time to time.

Jonn recovered from the Sickness but never regained the use of his leg as he'd hoped. His seizures did lessen considerably, possibly due to the mothkat bite. He was elected Mayor, and under his guidance, Iceliss flourished and grew.

Ann eventually sold Korr's house and returned to the Frost, and slowly, she was accepted into Iceliss once again. She refused numerous offers of courtship as she mourned Korr's death for two years, but eventually, I noticed that she began to linger at Jonn's side at parties and gatherings, listening to his ideas for the village and adding her own. Their romance grew quietly, and they were married shortly before the birth of my first daughter, Eloisa, a girl with hair and eyes as dark as her father's. My second daughter, Jonna, was born only a day before Jonn and Ann's son, Meridus, and they grew up as close as if they were twins, playing hand in hand in the Frost and whispering secrets at Assembly.

Ivy never married, and that suited her just fine. She remained the beloved aunt to Eloisa, Jonna, Meridus, and the soon-to-come-after little Camilla. Eccentric and playful, Ivy preferred the company of her Watchers to the rest of the world. She formed a school in the wilderness and took apprentices to learn the ways of the creatures that we'd once regarded as monsters. She grew wise and revered among the villagers, taking the name Keeper and forming a new legacy for herself that she passed on to the students she trained.

Borde had reprogrammed the gate to be able to return to the past, and our easy connection with Astralux was lost. Still, travel between the two locations grew steadily. Doctors and teachers came to Iceliss, and the village expanded. Frost dweller children went to university in Aeralis, and Aeralian students came to the Frost to study and learn about Echlos and the Watchers.

Aaron stayed in the Frost and, with time, he became a loving grandfather. His favorite pastime was regaling his grandchildren with stories of the Frost's ancient past and the amazing devices that had filled that place. They did not often believe him, I fear.

Over the years, Gabe and I gradually began to speak again, beginning with his greenhouse gift at my wedding. He did not marry, although he and Clara remained close friends and it was always rumored in Aeralian papers that they would soon wed. Adam encouraged me to mend the friendship, and I did so with his blessing. Gabe and I exchanged letters, and our closeness deepened as the rift between us healed. Gabe even visited us sometimes, to the delight of the entire village of Iceliss. Eloisa and Jonna especially loved to see him. Once we even traveled to Astralux to see him in his royal palace, and they were wide-eyed with wonder at the iron bridges and steamcoaches in the streets.

The winter that Eloisa turned twenty, Adam caught a fever that turned into pneumonia. He died in my arms. We buried him in the greenhouse, and I lived with the pain of not breathing for months until one day I could see color again, and my grief was bearable. Time healed me, but slowly.

Gabe's letters increased during my lonely widowed year following Adam's death, and one day in early spring, he surprised me in the Frost outside the farmyard, not far from the place where I'd first found him. He told me he was retiring from his place as ruler of Aeralis. The nation was transitioning to a republic, and he would live the rest of his days in peace.

He asked me again if I would marry him, because, he said, love is a perilous dance, but worth dancing all the same.

This time, I said yes.

ABOUT THE AUTHOR

Kate Avery Ellison lives in Atlanta, Georgia, with her husband and two spoiled (but extremely lovable) cats. She loves dark chocolate, fairy tale retellings, and love stories with witty banter and sizzling, unspoken feelings. When she isn't working on her next writing project, she can be found reading, watching one of her favorite TV shows, working on an endless list of DIY household projects, or hanging out with friends. She also loves hearing from readers!

You can find more information about Kate Avery Ellison's books and other upcoming projects online at http://thesouthernscrawl.blogspot.com/.

To be notified of new releases by Kate Avery Ellison, sign up for her New Releases Newsletter at http://thesouthernscrawl.blogspot.com/p/new-releases-newsletter.html, or "like" her on Facebook at https://www.facebook.com/kateaveryellison.

ACKNOWLEDGEMENTS

Scott, for being my life-long companion, tireless supporter, and first reader of every manuscript. I've already said this a zillion times, but I wouldn't have published a single book without your encouragement, so I'm forever in your debt for believing in me. I love you.

My family (my parents, siblings, and wonderful in-laws) for talking about my books to practically every person you meet in every doctor's office and classroom between here and North Carolina, for cheering me on, and for acting like I'm famous. I love you guys.

H. Danielle Crabtree, for being a wonderful editor (and a fan of the Frost). It's a true pleasure to work with you.

Charles, for your friendship, support, and enthusiasm. Thank you for proofing my manuscript, listening to me talk shop about writing, and being so darn excited about the stuff I do. You are the best friend.

Melissa, for providing encouragement in chats and threads, and for letting me blather endlessly about ideas and plans and finding them interesting. You are amazing. We are going to do great things together with our collective writing powers, I just know it.

Dru, Doug, Daniel, Sarah, and Mackenzie, for reading and saying nice things about the Frost Chronicles. You guys are awesome.

Thomas, because I'm sorry I didn't name a character after you and then make him a superhero like you asked. Maybe in the next book. It could have been worse, though. I could have named the villain Thomas.

My readers, for loving this world I've created enough to read five books about it. I love you all!